The Treasure of the Padres

HARPER & ROW, PUBLISHERS
NEW YORK, EVANSTON, AND LONDON

Weekly Reader Children's Book Club presen[...]

THE TREASURE OF THE PADRES

by BETTY BAKER

Pictures by LEONARD SHORTALL

THE TREASURE OF THE PADRES

Harper & Row, Publishers, Incorporated,
49 East 33rd Street, New York 16, N.Y.

Weekly Reader Children's Book Club Edition
Senior Division

Library of Congress catalog card number: 64-12027

for Susan,
who thought all Indians were skinny

CONTENTS

All places in this book are fictitious except the museum. The mystery of the bells is based on the missing ghost bells of the Mission of Tumacacori. All characters are fictitious except Bootsie.

The Treasure of the Padres

1

Things

The thermometer read one hundred and two in the shade, but it wasn't because of the heat that Tim sprawled on the metal lounge. So long as he stayed in the shade of the spreading mulberry tree or didn't exert himself too much, the slight breeze kept him comfortable. Or maybe it was the dry desert air. His shirt didn't stick to him, nor did his forehead bead with perspiration the way it did back home in California.

Across the hot concrete patio a striped ground squirrel swung on the drooping branch of a mesquite. When the branch slowed and stopped, the little squirrel bounded to the ground and back to the branch, setting it in motion again and creating his own private breeze.

Tim sighed and pulled the broad-brimmed hat over his eyes to shut out the sight. If he were just a little kid, he could join the squirrel, but he was too old for such games now. Besides, the branch didn't look strong enough to hold him. Rather than torture himself by watching he confined his view to the worn knees of his levis and the toes of his new cowboy boots. He wriggled them and sighed again.

He'd thought it would be so different when Mr. Perkins had first appeared at the Bowdy home last February.

"Have a ranch in Arizona," the wiry, weather-beaten man had said. "No kith nor kin, just a lot of old Indian doofunnies left me by my grandparents. Decided I'd leave something worthwhile behind me."

Then he'd rambled on about turning his ranch house into a museum and the foreman's house into a coffee shop.

"Folks'll come out to gawk and maybe stay

a spell. Gets a mite lonesome out there with only the Indians. Oh, those Papagos are right friendly and polite, but they don't run to loose jaws." He hunched forward. "Now, back a ways from the ranch house I got me an old Spanish mission."

Tim's father almost dropped his pipe at that. Though a busy architect, Mr. Bowdy's favorite work was restoring old Spanish buildings. He'd done several between Los Angeles and San Diego. Now Mr. Perkins had another.

"Don't give me an answer now," said the old rancher. "Think on it a spell. Can't be done 'til summer anyhow. Got to bed you in the foreman's house, and right now I got it rented to winter visitors."

That should have warned Tim. What working ranch rented its foreman's house? But the thought of spending a summer with horses, cowboys, and Indians overran his usual good judgment. Eagerly he awaited his father's decision.

Mr. Perkins made another trip to California. Tim begged, and at last Mr. Bowdy said Yes.

Then Mother had insisted on taking so many things along, they'd needed a little move-yourself trailer, and that meant putting a trailer hitch on the car. Then Debbie had made herself ill when the cat disappeared for three days. For a while Tim had feared they'd never be ready by the third week in June. But two days ago they'd driven into the Perkins ranch. Only then did Tim discover that the ranch was nothing but desert, and Mr. Perkins had even sold most of that. There were no horses, no cattle, no cowboys, and as far as Tim could see, no Indians either. Why, he hadn't even seen a jackrabbit or a coyote, though last night Mr. Perkins had killed a rattlesnake right here on the patio.

The screen door creaked and thudded. From under his hatbrim Tim watched Debbie's blue thongs flip-flop toward him. He made a bet with himself, pushed back his hat, and saw that he'd won. Bootsie was cradled in his sister's arms like a baby. It seemed Debbie couldn't go anywhere without that dumb cat.

"Aren't you supposed to be helping Mom unpack?" he asked.

"She said it's too hot to work for a while."

"You have the cooler on, don't you?"

"But it isn't as cool as the air conditioning at home. Besides, we're almost finished."

Debbie jounced and jiggled, settling herself on the other lounge, making Bootsie's four white paws wave limply as if in greeting.

Tim had never seen a cat that looked or acted so much like a fluffy, black-and-white teddy bear. Even the yellow eyes were round like the ones on stuffed toys, and the dumb cat was just as useless. Yet it was lazy Bootsie who'd discovered and tackled the rattlesnake last night. Tim had new respect for the cat. She had handled the rattler until Mr. Perkins came to the rescue.

"Why don't you let Bootsie run?" he asked.

"No." Debbie clutched her pet tighter. When the animal purred instead of struggling, Tim decided last night had been an accident. Bootsie was just a dumb cat after all. But there was nothing else to do here except annoy Debbie, so he tried again.

"It's too hot to hold her like that. You're making her suffer."

"She likes it. Besides, there might be *things* around." The girl shivered as she glanced at the nick the bullet had left in the concrete.

"If a rattler comes out in this sun, he'll burn up."

"How do you know?"

"Mr. Perkins told me. He said rattlers mostly come out at night. He's lived here all his life. So did his father and his grandfather, so he ought to know."

Debbie bit her lip thoughtfully. Then she opened her arms. Bootsie didn't move. She set the cat down on the patio. It rolled over on its back and yawned. Then it noticed the ground squirrel and padded across to investigate, the fat sidcs bouncing at every step. Tim tensed, ready to yell if Bootsie crouched to spring, but the cat watched a moment, then padded back and jumped into Debbie's arms.

"See there, Timothy Bowdy? You think you're so smart."

"At least I'm not a scarebaby afraid to move two feet from the house."

"I don't see you going anyplace."

"There's no place to go." Tim wished he were back home. Jack and Freddy and the rest were probably in someone's pool right now. Or maybe one of the mothers had driven them to Redondo Beach to fish. He couldn't even go to a movie here. The closest one was thirty miles away in Tucson.

Debbie said it out loud. "I wish I were back in Los Angeles." Then she added angrily, "I hate it here."

Tim stared at his sister. He was certainly bored, but he didn't hate the desert. "Why? What's wrong with this place?"

"What's wrong?" she shrieked. "You saw that snake last night. I'll bet it was ten feet long."

"Two feet three inches," Tim corrected. "Mr. Perkins and I skinned it this morning."

Debbie continued as if she hadn't heard. "There are scorpions and lizards and fire ants and all sorts of crawly things. I can't go off the patio in thongs because of the cactus, and the sun glares so badly it hurts my eyes."

Tim snorted. As if any of that really mattered.

"Besides," Debbie wailed, "there's nothing to do."

He agreed but saw no reason to admit it to Debbie. It was a matter of principle never to agree with her unless absolutely necessary. He eyed the toes of his boots.

"You could go Western," he suggested. "Then at least the cactus wouldn't hurt."

"I *am* Western. You can't go any farther west than California."

"What about Hawaii?"

"All right, smarty. Then what about China? That's west of Hawaii. And India's west of China, and Arabia's west of India." She giggled. "So the Near East is really the West."

"Fooferall."

"What?"

"Fooferall. That's what Mr. Perkins would say you've been talking." He swung his legs over the side of the lounge and sat up. "Speaking of

Mr. Perkins, I reckon I'll mosey yonder to the ranch house and see how my varmint skin's a-dryin', pardner."

"Oh, stop it."

"I'm just trying to get into the spirit of the Old West."

"I'll settle for the New West, thank you. Especially the part around Los Angeles." Debbie put her heels on the lounge seat and rested her chin on her knees. "Go ahead and see Mr. Perkins. Don't mind me."

Tim hesitated. She did look lonely.

"Want to come?" he asked.

"No! Those awful thorns stick to the soles of my thongs and then drop all over the bedroom floor. They're terrible to step on. Besides, there are *things* all over this desert."

"Fooferall. You're just a shadow-shy scarebaby."

Hc strolled between the leafless palo verde trees to the large ranch house where Mr. Perkins lived alone. The board on which they'd stretched the snakeskin lay on the long roofed porch. *Ramada,* Tim corrected mentally. That's what

Mr. Perkins called the porch, just as he often called the ranch house the *hacienda*.

The front door stood open, but there was no screen door. Tim rapped loudly on the door-frame.

"Come in and set," called a muffled voice.

Tim stepped into the dim room and blinked his eyes rapidly. The rancher was head and shoulders inside a deep cupboard.

"Be with you in a jiffy." There was rustling inside the cupboard, followed by a sneeze. "Blamed dust. Just drop the laundry anywhere."

"What laundry?"

Mr. Perkins crawled out backward and lifted a dusty face to Tim.

"Thought you were Maria's boy. Set down, Tim. Be right with you." He wiped the cobwebs from his grizzled whiskers and dove back into the cupboard.

Tim backed toward a seat, staring unbelievingly around the large, cool room. No wonder Mr. Perkins intended to make it into a museum. A pair of chairs made of long, twisted steer horns flanked a round corner fireplace plastered with adobe. More horns hung on the wall beside heads of deer, lions, and wild pigs. Large Navajo rugs covered the floor, the space between them filled by bear and calf skins. On one side, taking up as much room as a grand piano, was an honest-to-goodness buffalo, stuffed and mounted.

Awestruck, Tim lowered himself to the lumpy sofa. A mountain lion snarled at him over the arm. Tim jumped before he realized it, too, was stuffed and mounted.

Mr. Perkins, standing at last, chuckled. "Give you a start, did it? Don't have many visitors or I'd move it. As it is, I keep forgetting it's there."

How could anyone forget a full-sized, crouching mountain lion?

"Did you shoot all these?" Tim asked.

"No, not me. Never was much for hunting, lessen we needed meat and didn't want to give up a steer. No, some Britisher come out here in the eighties. Grandpa said that Britisher was just *loco* over shooting. Stuffed these himself, he did."

Mr. Perkins chuckled as he pointed at the

buffalo. "He got that out on the plains. Mounted it right on the spot and then dragged it along on a wagon. Caused a fair sensation, I can tell you."

"After all that trouble, didn't he want it?"

"Reckon he did. Howsomever, he left his rig and specimens, as he called these things, here with Grandpa while he went north to shoot some more. Met with Apaches, poor fella. Grandpa wrote his folks back in England, but they had no use for this stuff. Said to keep it and much obliged."

He rubbed his whiskers. "That old buffalo's a mite mangy now, but he'll smarten my museum a bit, don't you think?"

"It sure will."

Mangy or not, the round glass eyes looked vicious to Tim. He could almost imagine the beast straining to free itself from the heavy base. He shook his head angrily. Hc was getting as bad as Debbie. He noticed the pile of bows and arrows, quivers, axes, and other things at the rancher's feet.

"Can I help you, Mr. Perkins?"

"Why, that's kindly of you." He handed Tim a sheaf of papers covered with a spidery scrawl. "Every proper museum's got to have a list of everything in it. I'll call off these things and you write them down. Reckon you're handier at that than I am."

Tim settled himself cross-legged on a moth-eaten bearskin.

"Ready, Mr. Perkins."

"One Apache tomahawk, two Cheyenne. One Navajo medicine bag, empty. One bone scraper, origin unknown." The rancher winked at Tim. "How you like that professional lingo? Learned it from those archaeological fellers from the museum that are always prowling and poking around these parts."

Tim gazed at the surrounding piles of Indian wares. "I'll bet they'd like to have this collection."

"Don't reckon they'd turn it down if I should offer, but this stuff isn't what they're looking for. Those museum people are after real old things. Stumbled on one old cave out on the reservation and now they're hot-footed to find another. Well, let's get on with it."

The dusty shelves and cupboards seemed bottomless. Tim ceased to be amazed at the assortment of Indian relics. He wrote quickly and automatically until Mr. Perkins interrupted a listing of baskets to call out, "One clumsy finger."

"One what?" Tim looked up expecting to see a real finger or at least a bone. Mr. Perkins held out a round, flat basket, the white background turned brown with age.

"Clumsy Finger we always called it. Some old Papago gave it to Grandma. Told her it was valuable, and I reckon it is. Never saw one so messed up."

Even Tim could see that the basketmaker must either have had ten thumbs or been blind. The design was off balance—cramped in one place and then stretched to fill the leftover space. And the two sides didn't even match.

"Maria has conniptions whenever she sees

this," Mr. Perkins went on. "She's the best basketmaker on the reservation. She thinks our Clumsy Finger should be burned. Reckon that's what makes it so valuable, it being the only example around of a Papago that couldn't make decent baskets. When I get my new cases, I'm giving old Clumsy Finger an honored place no matter how Maria fusses and frets."

He laid the Clumsy Finger gently on the growing mound. Then he leaned forward, squinting at the open door. Tim twisted around to see what he was staring at.

It was Debbie, her head swiveling this way and that, peering at the ground. Once she turned clear around to look behind her.

"What's she expecting to find?" asked the rancher. "Gold?"

Tim grinned. "She's looking for snakes and afraid she'll find one. Oh-oh!"

Behind the girl the tall peppergrass bent and swayed. One of Debbie's *things* was stalking her, creeping closer and closer to the shuffling thongs.

2

Stuffy

Tim opened his mouth to yell a warning, then grinned instead. Out of the peppergrass wriggled a black-and-white animal. It crouched. The tip of the fluffy tail twitched nervously. Round yellow eyes watched the sandals move almost to the ramada. Bootsie's rear shimmied, and the cat leaped at Debbie's right ankle. Debbie screamed, took the wide porch in one jump, and plunged into the room only to scream again as she came face to face with the buffalo. Tim rolled on the floor howling and clutching his aching sides.

"It isn't funny, Timothy Bowdy," she yelled.

"No, it isn't," agreed Mr. Perkins, but he looked as if he was having trouble keeping his mouth turned down. "Now you just set a spell and calm yourself, young lady. Is that animal yours?"

Bootsie sat outside the door calmly washing the ruffled fur.

"Yes, but she won't be mine long if she does that again."

"Bootsie wouldn't claw you." Tim glanced at Debbie's ankle and went into fresh peals of laughter. He pointed at her feet. "You jumped clear out of your thongs, scarebaby."

She pretended not to hear, but from the way she bit her lip Tim knew her temper was building. She'd be mean and contrary all day now. Maybe tomorrow, too, though she spoke sweetly enough to Mr. Perkins.

"Mother wants to know if we may move some things in the storage room to make space for our empty packing cartons."

"Go right ahead. Nothing in there of any account that I know of."

"Thank you." She rose stiffly, shot Tim a

just-you-wait look, and stalked out to retrieve her thongs. As she pushed her toes through the straps she stared off past the house.

"There's someone coming, Mr. Perkins. He's riding."

"That'll be Maria's boy with my laundry. Come along, Tim. I want you two to meet."

Tim needed no urging to follow the rancher outside. A chubby boy guided a large brown animal, with black mane and tail, around the empty corrals and up toward the house.

"I never saw a horse like that before," said Tim.

"Reckon you never will either," said Mr. Perkins. "That's a mule. Didn't you notice the jackrabbit ears?"

Debbie giggled. Tim flushed and glanced at the drying snakeskin, a dozen possibilities flickering in his mind.

The mule stopped a few feet from the ramada. Mr. Perkins stepped forward and took the bundle the boy handed down.

"Don't know what I'd do without your ma. If I'd have knowed what a bother all this washing and cooking can be, I'd never have hung up my saddle."

There was no saddle on the mule. The boy rode bareback. When he slid to the ground, Tim saw the boy was nearly a head shorter than himself and so stocky his levis had no place to rest securely. The boy hitched them up and glanced shyly from Debbie to Tim.

"Glad you come just now," said the rancher. "Want you to meet Tim and Debbie Bowdy. This here's Ramón Ramirez."

"But everybody calls me Stuffy." He patted his bulging stomach and grinned.

"Does he bite?" asked Debbie.

"Course not," said Mr. Perkins. "There's a limit even to what Stuffy eats." And he chuckled as he took his laundry into the house.

Debbie didn't so much as smile. She clutched Bootsie in her arms and stared big-eyed at the mule.

"Chiquita's very gentle," Stuffy assured her.

The mule stretched its neck toward the cat and flubbered through black lips. Debbie yelped and jumped backward.

"Chiquita won't hurt you," Stuffy repeated.

"Don't pay any attention to Debbie," said Tim. "She's just a scarebaby."

"I am not."

Tim ignored her. "Do you live near here, Stuffy?"

"Just over there on the reservation about five miles."

"Then you must be an Indian."

Stuffy nodded. He looked worried but smiled again when Tim shouted, "Debbie, did you hear that? Stuffy's a real, honest-to-goodness real live Indian."

"He is not."

The smile vanished from the round brown face. "But I am."

"No, you're not," said Debbie firmly. "Indians are tall and thin with high cheekbones. You're too fat to be an Indian."

"I guess I do stuff myself too much." He felt his sides.

"Besides," continued Debbie, "your nose is all wrong. No Indian has a pug nose."

Stuffy felt his nose as if he'd just discovered he had one. "But I look just like my father and mother, and they're Papagos. I know they are. My father couldn't be a policeman on the reservation of he wasn't."

"Then the Papagos aren't Indians."

"Not Indians?" Stuffy twisted the reins in his hands. "But if the Papagos aren't Indians, what are they?"

Debbie shrugged. "How should I know? But they can't be Indians."

"Don't listen to her fooferall," Tim said. "She'll talk you in circles until you don't know your own name. Just a while ago she tried to tell me that Arabia was really the West. She proved it too."

Stuffy looked even more bewildered. "But in school we learned that–"

"I know," Tim interrupted. "And Debbie knows, but she's feeling so ornery today that nothing suits her; so she's changing the whole world to please herself. Pay no attention to her."

"You think you're so smart, Timothy Bowdy. I'll ask Dad tonight. He'll tell you Stuffy's not an Indian."

She swung toward home, still carefully looking for *things*. He hoped she'd find one. He could see her plaid shirt through the branches of the palo verde tree where she had stopped to hear what the boys were saying.

Mr. Perkins poked his head out the door. "Why don't you boys ride out to the mission? See how Tim's pa is coming along?"

Stuffy ducked his head shyly. "I couldn't ask Tim to ride bareback on a slow old mule like Chiquita."

"Sure you could," Tim said quickly. "And I'd say Yes, so let's go."

Without stirrups they had to lead Chiquita to the corral and climb the rails to mount. As soon as Tim settled behind Stuffy, the Indian boy kicked the mule's sweaty sides and she plodded off.

"Bring me a full report," Mr. Perkins yelled.

Tim waved. "I will." Though with Mr.

Bowdy still just making sketches, he didn't see what he'd have to report.

The desert shimmered under the hot sun. Chiquita moved easily through the sparse growth–mesquite, cholla, barrel cactus, ocotillo, and here and there one of the giant saguaros, the tall sentinel cactus of the Arizona desert. Tim slapped his thighs happily, unafraid of falling from Chiquita's broad back. Calabasas, Tubac, Pete Kitchen's ranch, Topawa, Bitter Wells, Growler Pass–all the names he'd read and heard about–sang in his ears. This was the very land where Apaches, Mexicans, and United States cavalry had fought. Only the Papagos were left; but the desert, pierced by brooding, jagged peaks, had a sinister haunted look as if waiting for ghost armies to appear and refight the old battles.

Tim shivered and Stuffy asked over his shoulder, "Is something wrong?"

"No, just that it's sort of spooky." Tim forced himself to laugh.

Stuffy nodded. "A land as old as this holds many spirits."

"You're kidding." But the Indian's voice hadn't sounded as if he were joking. "You don't really believe there are ghosts out here?"

"Not ghosts. Spirits."

Tim snorted. "They're the same thing."

"Perhaps, but I don't believe so. You just said it felt spooky. That's a spirit. Sort of a feeling, like sometimes you ride into a canyon and feel it's an evil place where something bad might happen. Another canyon almost like it will feel like a good place to camp."

"You're talking about hunches, not spirits." For a minute Tim had been afraid that Stuffy was as big a scarebaby as Debbie.

"Perhaps." Stuffy was silent a moment. "Perhaps also the stories have something to do with it. The Old Ones had stories about every peak and canyon. That one, way over there, is Baboquivari. It was once the sacred mountain of the Papagos and can be seen from anywhere on the reservation. Near it is a hole in the rock where Se'ehe is said to have pushed evil Ho'ok into the ground."

A cone-shaped hill, topped by a split peak,

stood alone in the desert just ahead. Tim knew the mission was at its base. He reached over Stuffy's shoulder to point.

"What's the name of that one?"

"Two Sisters, for the double peaks on top." He turned to grin at Tim. "That's a love story."

"You can tell that one to Debbie."

Even at Chiquita's stumbling gait they were soon following the dirt road up the hillside to the mission. The crumbling building was similar to dozens Tim had seen before. A courtyard large enough to hold three more missions was surrounded by adobe walls five feet thick. They had kept out Apaches but not the tumbleweed. The courtyard was filled with the big ball-shaped plants. Many were three feet high and as big around as a barrel. The curving green stems were bare except for the thorny seeds.

Two pickup trucks and a horse stood outside the gap were the gate had once been.

"I wonder who's here," said Tim.

"Men from the reservation. I know the trucks."

"Dad must be hiring men."

Before they could dismount, Mr. Bowdy strode through the gateway. "Hello there, Tim. What are you doing out here?"

"Mr. Perkins wanted a report. Dad, this is Stuffy Ramirez."

Mr. Bowdy pushed back his hat and looked up at Stuffy. "Ramirez, you say? Is your father on the reservation police force?"

"Yes, sir."

"I met him yesterday. A fine man." He looked at Tim. "Sorry I can't talk now, son. I'm very busy."

"That's all right. We really came just for the ride."

"And we must get right back," Stuffy added, looking anxiously at the lowering sun.

"What shall I tell Mr. Perkins?"

"I'll see him myself in an hour or so. But tell your Mother to get the camping gear together. We start real work tomorrow."

He waved, and Stuffy turned Chiquita back down the hill.

After a long silence Stuffy said, "Is your father going to camp here at the mission?"

"Yes, he and the men he's hiring. Mr. Perkins said they live so far out on the reservation that work will go faster if they camp here and go home weekends. Otherwise they'll waste hours traveling every day."

"I do not think so."

"Why? Aren't the Indians scattered on farms?"

"Yes, but that is not what I meant. I meant that I do not think anyone will stay after dark at the mission." Stuffy's voice lowered to a whisper. "The ranchers once used the courtyard as a holding corral for cattle branding. Suddenly they stopped. Even Mr. Perkins has never camped here since. He never said why, but surely he heard it."

"Heard what?" In spite of himself Tim was whispering too.

"The bell," said Stuffy softly. "The ghost bell of San Raphael Mission."

3

A Disappearance

Shadows lay long and mysterious across the desert. The tall saguaros, dark against the sky, looked like invaders from another planet. Behind them Two Sisters was blue-shadowed, the peaks tipped pink by the slanted rays of the sun. The eerie landscape and Stuffy's low voice made the story of the ghost bell almost real.

"When the Spanish padres came to our people over two hundred years ago, we helped them to build the Mission of San Raphael. A great bell was brought from Mexico and hung in the belfry. Now all are gone: padres, belfry, and bell."

"What happened?"

Stuffy hesitated, then said slowly, "The Indians attacked. The padres fled to Mexico. The bell was too large for them to have carried it on foot across the desert, but when our people returned to the mission the bell was gone. Some say that the evil Ho'ok returned and stole it. Others say the Apaches destroyed it, but no trace has even been found. But at night, in the ruined mission, the bell has been heard."

"Who heard it?" Tim couldn't let himself believe such a tale. Somehow he had to break the spell the desert twilight had thrown over him.

"My grandfather heard it ring. Others have also."

Tim snorted. "And I suppose when the ghost bell rings, calamity and death are sure to follow."

"Perhaps. I have never heard that, but it may be true."

No doubt the next time Stuffy told the story, he'd add the bit about misfortune following the peal of the bell. That just proved how all nonsense about ghosts started in the first place. It also proved that Stuffy was as shadow-shy as Debbie. How could Tim be friends with anyone silly enough to believe in ghosts? And a bell at that. If it were a six-eyed monster or a headless horseman, it wouldn't be so bad. But a bell!

Then Tim remembered Stuffy was an Indian. He had a right to be more superstitious than other people. Besides, Stuffy had only told the story. He hadn't said he believed it. By the time Chiquita wheezed to a stop by the patio, Tim was again enthused about his new friendship.

"Can you come over tomorrow?" he asked Stuffy.

"If you want me to."

"Sure I do. Same time?"

"The afternoons are a little hot. I have chores to do, but I'll get up early tomorrow. Perhaps I will be here by ten. Is that all right?"

"Fine. I'll ask Mom to pack a picnic lunch. I mean, if you and Chiquita don't mind riding again." He glanced at the sky. "It's going to be dark in a minute. If you wait, Dad will take you home. You can tie Chiquita to the trailer hitch."

But he frowned doubtfully. Could Dad possibly drive slow enough for the mule?

"It's all right. I'm often out after dark. Chiquita always knows the way home. It's the only time she moves faster than a walk." He waved. *"Hasta mañana."*

"Until tomorrow," repeated Tim.

A voice behind him warned, "Are you going to get it, Timothy Bowdy."

Tim whirled to find Debbie lurking in the shadows. "Stop sneaking up like that."

"I didn't sneak. I just came to tell you Mom's been looking all over for you. She wanted you to put those packing boxes in the storage room."

His heart sank. He hated to worry his mother —especially since she always got mad whenever she found out there'd been nothing to worry about.

"Why didn't you tell her I'd gone with Stuffy? You heard us. I saw you eavesdropping behind the palo verde."

"Why should I run your errands?"

Tim leaned close and hissed, "Watch out!

It's almost dark and the *things* are out!"

He had to jump out of her path as she dashed to the house. He glanced over at Mr. Perkins' house. The snakeskin was still on the old rancher's ramada. It would have to wait until morning. He'd better go right in to Mom. Much as he dreaded it, he'd better get it over with before he asked about going riding with Stuffy again tomorrow.

But all his mother said was, "I'm glad you're back. Another few minutes and I'd have worried. Did your father hire his crew?"

Tim stared at her. "How did you know where I was?"

"Debbie told me. You asked her to, remember?" She laughed. "Don't tell me this desert sun is affecting your memory."

Tim clenched his fists and wished he'd remembered that snakeskin. It would serve Debbie right to wake up tomorrow and find it stretched out beside her bed. She had told Mom where he'd gone, as she always did, but she couldn't resist worrying him. How long would it take her to get out of this ornery mood?

Mrs. Bowdy gathered up an armful of shirts and socks. "This is the last, thank goodness. Tim, would you please put those boxes in the storage room?"

One of the waist-high cartons lay on its side. Tim grabbed the edge and felt weight inside. It was Bootsie. She lay as far back as she could get, contentedly ripping the packing paper to shreds. Tim shook the carton.

"Come on out, you dumb cat."

Another piece of paper ripped. Tim reached in. Soft paws batted his hand playfully. Then the cat moved into a corner out of reach. Tim tapped his fingers on the edge of the box. Yellow eyes watched the moving fingers. The rear shimmied. The cat pounced and Tim grabbed, ruffled the long fur, and pushed the cat gently to one side.

"Go get Debbie to play with you. I have work to do."

Whistling softly he carried two cartons through the kitchen to the storage room. It was the one place Tim hadn't yet explored. His whistle rose and fell in amazement.

The small house had only two bedrooms. Tim had to share one with Debbie. This storage room was large enough to make a third small bedroom, but where, Tim wondered, would he put all this junk? Much as he hated sharing a room with his sister and her dumb cat, he wouldn't begin to try cleaning this place.

Shelves and hooks ranged three walls, all loaded with ragged clothes, bent pails, cast-off harness, strings of dried peppers, empty bottles, baskets, and lumpy objects near the ceiling too covered with dust to identify. Huge brown jars shared the floor with broken rawhide chairs, steer horns, kegs, and an old dress form draped in a torn *serape*. Tim had just cleared a space large enough to stack the cartons when he heard his father in the kitchen.

"The men won't camp at the mission," Mr. Bowdy was saying. "They're willing to come after dawn and work, but they insist on leaving well before dark."

Debbie giggled. "Don't tell me they think the mission is haunted."

"Debbie's right." Tim stepped into the kitchen. "Stuffy was telling me about it."

Mr. Bowdy ruffled Tim's hair. "Is there some dreadful Apache spirit roaming the courtyard seeking vengeance?" he asked.

"No, it's not an Indian. Guess again."

"Some kind of monster," said Debbie with a shiver. "And it's probably *real*."

"Wrong again."

His mother turned from stirring something on the stove. "Surely it isn't the ghost of one of those old Jesuit priests?"

"No, but you're getting closer." Tim paused to let the suspense build, then said softly, "It's the bell."

"A ghost bell?" Debbie giggled. "Fooferall."

Tim stared at his sister. "Aren't you scared?"

"Not of a bell. That's silly."

"I agree," said Mr. Bowdy. "But some of the Papagos I hired live quite far out on the reservation. If they have to travel back and forth every day, this job will take a lot longer than we thought."

"Then we'll be here when school opens," wailed Debbie.

"There you go," said Tim. "Always thinking about yourself. What about Mr. Perkins? He won't have everything ready for the winter season."

"Besides costing him much more than he planned," added Mr. Bowdy. "Of course he can always sell some of his collection."

"He couldn't," said Tim. "What would be the use of having a museum then?"

Debbie looked on the verge of tears. Her father gave her a quick hug.

"Cheer up, Debbie," he said. "We won't worry until the time comes." As they settled around the table he added, "Maybe Stuffy and his father could help persuade the other Indians that there's nothing to this ghost-bell story."

Tim thought Debbie's mood had changed, but once his sister took hold of an idea, she never let go.

"Stuffy's not an Indian," she declared. "He's too fat and his face is the wrong shape."

She gave Tim a triumphant look. For a minute Tim almost believed she was right, but then Mr. Bowdy laughed.

"You're thinking of the plains Indians, like the Cheyenne. The Papagos are different, just as the French and Norwegians are different."

"You mean the French are small and dark, while the Norsemen are tall and blond?"

"That's it exactly, but remember that there are also many Frenchmen and Norwegians who don't look that way at all."

"You mean that's just the way we think of them," said Tim. "Just like Debbie thinks all Indians should look like the Cheyenne. I'll bet some of the Cheyenne don't look like that either."

"No, they don't. Now tell me what Stuffy said about this mysterious bell."

Tim repeated the little that Stuffy had told him. Mr. Bowdy nodded from time to time, then sighed wistfully.

"It would certainly help if that bell could be found. According to the old church records I had copied in Mexico, that bell was a collector's item. It was cast in Spain almost seven hundred years ago and can't be duplicated today. Having it for the new belfry would certainly make Mr. Perkins' mission one of the most authentic around, except for San Xavier."

"Why don't you advertise for information?" suggested Mrs. Bowdy. "You have a complete description of the bell from the old records. Some miner or a wagon train might have hauled it away. Remember that one mission bell you discovered in an old mining-town schoolhouse? Something as large as a bell can't just vanish."

"This one did," said Tim. "Or so Stuffy says."

His mother glanced at the clock. "It's getting late, Tim. I thought I asked you to put those cartons away."

He gulped the last of his milk and pushed back his chair. "I'll do it right now, Mom."

He carried the last cartons into the storage room and stacked them to the ceiling. They

wobbled unsteadily. He couldn't leave them like that. Wiping his face on his sleeve, he began clearing more floor space. Behind a keg of worn horseshoes he found a guitar with one string. After rearranging the cartons in smaller stacks and putting an odd one on top of an empty flour barrel, he sat down on the floor with the guitar. He was so busy trying to vary the tone by holding the one string against the different ridges that he forgot the time.

"Timothy," his mother called. "What are you doing in there? It's time for bed."

He gave the string one last twang and shut the door behind him. He yawned and rubbed his legs. Too much riding and climbing up and down after cartons. Sleepily he muttered good night to his parents and headed for the room he shared with Debbie.

Mr. Bowdy had hung a bamboo curtain across the center of the room so each of them had a private section. As Tim dropped his shirt and levis on the floor Debbie yelled from the other side of the bamboo.

"Don't you dare leave those clothes in here, Timothy Bowdy. They smell."

"They do not."

"They do too. Look at them." A bare foot kicked under the screen. "They're covered with mule hair and they smell like a stable."

"That's a good clean smell."

"Mother!" she screeched. "Tim's smelling up the whole room with his old mule clothes. I won't be able to sleep a wink."

Mr. Bowdy came to the door. "Better put those jeans in the bathroom, Tim. They are a little strong."

As Tim stomped through the hall Dad added, "The Papago are a very peaceful and courteous people. Maybe being with Stuffy this summer will do some good."

"I don't see how," said Tim. "Debbie isn't going with us. She's too much of a scarebaby to ride a mule."

Dad humphed the way he did when he'd explained an arithmetic problem twice and Tim still didn't understand.

Angrily Tim dumped the clothes in a corner

of the bathroom. He'd waste a lot of time getting dressed tomorrow on account of Debbie.

"You just better keep that dumb cat out of my way," he warned her.

"Bootsie doesn't bother you."

"She wakes me up before dawn every morning. I've stood for it long enough. Now you just better keep her on your own side of the curtain tomorrow, or else."

He bounced into bed. In spite of the heat he pulled the sheet over his head. Not that it helped much to drown out her defense of that dumb cat. For the hundredth time Tim wondered if Bootsie was really addled or if Debbie made her that way. Debbie was enough to muddy-brain anyone.

Afraid of cactus, afraid of snakes, afraid of an old mule, and now she yelled about a little smell. From now on he'd just pretend he didn't have a sister. He wouldn't even listen to her anymore.

But when Debbie shook him awake in the morning, her face wet with tears, Tim forgot his resolution.

"Bootsie's gone," Debbie told him.

"She'll come back. She did before, or didn't you think of that?"

"But she didn't go out. I fed her at suppertime and nobody let her out after that. When she didn't come to bed with me, I thought she was with Mom, but she hadn't seen Bootsie all evening."

"Oh, for criminy's sake. If she isn't outside, then she's inside. Even you have brains enough to figure that out."

He pulled the sheet over his head and turned his back to her. She tugged his shoulder.

"She isn't, Tim. Mom and Dad helped me look. Bootsie isn't anywhere in the house. She's disappeared." Debbie began to sob.

"Now stop that. Just think instead of throwing a fit." He sat up and scratched his head. "I was in the storage room last night. Maybe I shut Bootsie in there. You know how she crawls into any dark corner she finds. She was inside one of the cartons yesterday. She's probably in the storage room right now."

"We looked there," Debbie wailed. "We looked and looked and called and called. Something has taken her." She burst into a fresh flood of tears.

Tim snorted. "What could steal a cat from inside a house? One of your *things?*"

Debbie lifted her chin defiantly. "Go ahead and laugh, Timothy Bowdy, but there are so many awful things around here that anything could happen. I'm frightened."

"Scarebaby," Tim said automatically, but he was beginning to feel a little nervous himself. If neither Mom nor Dad had let Bootsie outside and no one could find the cat inside, where was she?

4

An Old Deerskin

Debbie brought Tim's clothes from the bathroom, holding them at arm's length and dropping them on a heap by the bed. Then she retreated to her side of the curtain while Tim dressed. She listed aloud all the things, possible and impossible, that might have happened to Bootsie. What an imagination! She still hadn't reached the end of the disasters by the time Tim got to his boots.

"Will you stop that?" he called. "I never heard such a scarebaby."

"Stop calling me that."

"Well, you are. You even make up things just to scare yourself silly."

The voice from behind the curtain rose higher. "I suppose you've never been scared."

"No." Sometimes he worried and there were occasions, like the first time he climbed the high dive, that made him nervous, but he'd never been really frightened the way Debbie seemed to get. There wasn't any sense in throwing fits the way she did. "There's always something you can do if you just stop to figure things out. You don't take time to think."

"But sometimes you can't think. Like when that rattlesnake was trying to kill Bootsie. Maybe another one got into the house and ate her."

"There's no crack or hole big enough for a rattler to get in the house. That's what I mean about thinking."

"There are some times when you're just too scared to think," she insisted.

"I haven't run across one yet."

He didn't wait for breakfast. He had to see for himself that Bootsie wasn't in the house. He turned the place upside down and found nothing. Debbie trailed him from room to room, wrinkling her nose in distaste at the dust Tim stirred up in the storage room. Though he searched behind and inside every carton, barrel, basket, and jar, he found no round-eyed cat. He climbed on the wobbly table, scanned the middle shelves, and jumped down.

"Aren't you going to look behind that stuff?" asked Debbie.

He shook his head. "If Bootsie went along there, she'd have left tracks. The dust is so thick and smooth, I don't think anything's been moved up there since Mr. Perkins' grandfather lived here."

She followed him into the kitchen and slumped across the table while he gulped orange juice and poured cereal into a bowl.

"All right, smarty," she demanded. "Where *is* Bootsie?"

"Give me time to think. She has to be somewhere. She couldn't just vanish into thin air."

"That bell from the mission did. Maybe the same thing happened to Bootsie."

Mrs. Bowdy patted her shoulder. "Your

father will help to look again this evening. Don't worry. We'll find Bootsie."

"Dead or alive." The words popped out before Tim could stop them. Debbie burst into tears. "Oh, for criminy's sake. It's a wonder you don't drown."

He pushed aside the cereal and stalked out to the ramada. He couldn't think with all that wailing. Besides, it was nine thirty and Stuffy would be coming soon. Tim dragged a chair to the end of the long porch where he could see out across the desert.

The ground squirrel sat up and inspected Tim, then scampered off. Tim glanced at the patio half expecting to see Bootsie rolling on the scratchy concrete. He could almost hear the dumb cat meowing.

He stood up and held his breath. Had he imagined it or did he really hear Bootsie? There it was again.

Tim looked up. The roof of the ramada was made of long, thin sticks plastered with adobe. It would be easy for a cat to climb along. It was also thick enough to muffle the cries.

"Bootsie," he called softly.

Another pitiful meow floated down. Tim dragged the chair off the porch. Bootsie must be on the roof. It wasn't high. When Tim stood on the chair, his eyes were level with the roof's edge. Nothing moved on it but a large hairy spider. The house roof was a foot higher and rimmed with a low adobe wall. Maybe the cat was there.

"Bootsie," he called again. "Kitty, kitty Bootsie."

He could almost feel his ears cocking like a dog's as he strained to catch the faintest sound, but there was nothing to hear except bird calls and the sighing of the wind. He was getting as bad as Debbie, jumping headlong without thinking. If Bootsie hadn't been let out last night, she couldn't possibly be on the roof.

Tim climbed down. Debbie stood on the porch, watching wide-eyed.

"What were you doing?" she asked.

"Catching spiders. There's one up there as big as my hand. You want it?"

"No!" She pointed toward the desert. "Here comes Stuffy."

Tim ran in to tell his mother and to ask for a picnic lunch. When he came out, Debbie was hopping up and down at the end of the porch.

"Timothy Bowdy, Bootsie's up there on the roof. You were going to ride off and leave her there."

"She's not up there."

"She is too. I heard her."

"I looked and she isn't there. Want me to boost you up so you can see for yourself?"

She put one foot on the chair and then must have remembered the spider. "No, thank you. I'll ask Stuffy to look."

"He's no taller than you are. He can't see from that chair."

"He can stand on Chiquita."

Tim stepped away from the building and measured it with his eyes. If Stuffy stood on the mule, he could even see over the rim of the house roof. That would prove once and for all that Bootsie wasn't up there.

Debbie stayed safely on the porch, but she

didn't wait for the mule to stop before she was babbling the story of Bootsie's disappearance.

"So will you stand up on Chiquita and get Bootsie off the roof? Please?" she finished breathlessly.

Tim opened his mouth and then shut it. If he said he'd already looked and the roof was empty, Debbie would only think he was trying to tell Stuffy to leave the cat up there.

"I'll hold the mule for you," he offered.

Stuffy grinned. "Don't worry about Chiquita. She doesn't move one step unless she must. But you could pull off my boots. That is, if you don't mind."

"You take that one, Debbie." When she didn't move, he shouted, "Come on, scarebaby. It's your cat. The least you can do for Stuffy is pull off a boot."

She circled way around Chiquita's head and inched up to Stuffy's leg. The mule looked back and flubbered. Debbie jumped. Tim roared.

"It's nothing," Stuffy said softly. "Chiquita's just curious. She thinks maybe you will kick her or pull hairs from her tail."

"I wouldn't do that."

Stuffy lifted his chubby shoulders in a shrug. "But how is Chiquita to know? So she looks to be sure."

Debbie chewed her lower lip. "You mean *she's* afraid of *me?*"

"Perhaps. Until she knows you better."

Debbie moved forward more confidently. Tim snorted and grabbed the heel of Stuffy's right boot. Mollycoddling Debbie that way. Why, she'd get over being afraid of Chiquita and then nothing would stop her from tagging along with the boys.

"You're watching the wrong end," he called to Debbie. "Mules don't bite. They kick."

He was too busy tugging and yanking at the boot to notice if his warning had any effect. At last the boot came free. Tim staggered backward and wiped his forehead on his sleeve.

"Your boots are even tighter than mine."

Stuffy sighed. "I'm getting too fat again. I always grow out of my clothes this way." He held his hands out from his sides.

Debbie held the other boot. Stuffy pulled his

legs up and knelt on Chiquita's broad back. Slowly he rose to a crouch, edging his feet under his body and balancing on his toes. Debbie was gnawing her lower lip to ribbons, but once his feet were firmly planted on the bare back, Stuffy stood up as calmly as if he were on the ground.

"Well?" said Debbie impatiently.

"I see nothing but a tarantula. He's a big one, too."

"A tarantula?" shrieked Debbie. "They're poisonous."

"No more than a bee or a wasp. Sometimes they are good to have around." He dropped quickly astride the mule, swung one leg over the back, and slid to the ground. "There is no cat anywhere on the roof."

"Not even on the house?" asked Tim.

Stuffy shook his head. "I am sorry, Debbie."

As he tugged on his boots Mrs. Bowdy stepped onto the porch with a plate of cookies and three paper cups of milk. Tim quickly introduced her to the Indian boy. His mother smiled.

"Hello, Stuffy. These two hardly ate any breakfast this morning. I'm sure you're hungry by now too."

The boy patted himself above the band of his levis. "Well, I'm a little stuffed."

Debbie giggled and Tim laughed. Stuffy grinned sheepishly.

"I'm sure you can find room for a few cookies," said Mrs. Bowdy. "Let me know when you leave, Tim," she called over her shoulder.

As they munched they discussed the mystery of the missing cat.

"I know I heard her." Debbie gazed up at the ceiling as if she expected Bootsie to be clinging there like a bat.

"I thought I did too," Tim said. "But she isn't up there."

Stuffy reached for his fourth cookie. "What kind of ceilings do you have inside?"

Tim frowned. What kind of a silly question was that? It had nothing to do with Bootsie, but Tim answered politely.

"The regular kind. Why?"

"This was the old ranch house. Big beams were used for the roof and they were left open. Mr. Perkins did a lot of work here when he decided to rent it. If he closed over the beams, there would be big spaces left between them."

"Big enough for a cat to crawl into," cried Tim.

Stuffy nodded and reached for another cookie. It was the last on the plate. He drew his hand away quickly.

"Take it, Stuffy," Debbie urged. "You need energy to help you think. *Some* people around here just *talk* about thinking."

"Then suppose you figure out how Bootsie could get through the ceiling." Tim stalked off and fed the last of his cookie to Chiquita.

Stuffy looked anxiously from Tim to Debbie. "But Tim couldn't know about the ceilings. If he had known about them, I'm sure he would have thought of it long ago."

"Save your breath," Tim said. "You couldn't sweeten Debbie with a barrelful of molasses."

Something clicked in his mind.

"That's it," he shouted.

Not stopping to explain, he rushed through the kitchen to the storage room. Debbie followed on his heels. Stuffy panted along behind, mumbling apologies to Mrs. Bowdy for tracking up her kitchen. Tim explained as he pulled down the stack of cartons.

"The barrel made me think of this corner. See the beams up there? This is where they join the ones over the kitchen and the rest of the house. The spaces between them were never closed. Bootsie could jump from this barrel to this carton, to another carton, to that top shelf near the ceiling. That's why there were no paw prints on the lower shelves."

They tugged and pushed the horseshoe barrel into the corner. Stuffy found a board to lay across it. Debbie put a chair on top of that.

"Couldn't you find one with a seat?" complained Tim.

Stuffy handed over another board and Tim slid it onto the chair, where the seat should have been. Debbie chewed her lip and looked sideways at Tim.

"Who's going to climb up?" she asked.

"It's your cat." Tim grinned at her terrified inspection of the makeshift ladder. "But I'm the tallest, so I'll do it."

The dust on the top shelf was scuffed and ridged. Paw prints showed clearly where Bootsie had investigated an overturned paint can.

"She's been up here, all right."

"Can you see her?" Debbie asked.

Tim didn't bother answering. The dust was scuffed only part way down the shelf. Bootsie must have come back and crawled between the beams, as Stuffy had suggested. Unless the cat swung like an acrobat there was only one space she could have gone into. Tim had worried about getting the cat to come out backward, but the huge beams were ten inches high with more than two feet between them. There was plenty of room for Bootsie to turn around. Tim shifted to a firmer stand and peered into the dark.

"Bootsie?"

Something stirred way back.

"Kitty, kitty Bootsie."

A chirrup answered him. It wasn't a meow or

a purr but the squirrellike sound in between that Bootsie used as an invitation to play. It always annoyed Tim when the cat woke him with it in the morning. Now it made him furious.

"That dumb cat!"

"She is not," Debbie yelled.

"I don't know what else you'd call her. She's stuck above the ceiling and all she wants to do is play. I don't think she wants out at all."

His sister's face puckered. Stuffy patted her arm.

"Don't worry," he soothed. "Tim will get your cat for you."

"Not if I have to crawl in after her, I won't." Yesterday he'd tricked Bootsie out of the carton, but now the cat was too far back. She might not see Tim's hand. To reach the cat Tim needed a stick.

Something in the corner of the opening caught his eye. A long tube of rolled brown leather was wedged between the top of the beam and the original roof. Tim would never have noticed it if one end hadn't been sticking out. From the way it was chewed, Bootsie had already been playing with it. The roll was stiff enough for Tim to thrust it back toward the faint stirrings.

He poked and wiggled the roll. Something batted the far end. Tim drew the tube a bit forward, wriggled it until Bootsie pounced, then again drew the tube toward himself. Bit by bit he lured the cat out. Soon he could see the gleaming round eyes following the movements of the leather roll. On the next pounce Tim grabbed the cat and drew her out.

"Bootsie!" Debbie reached eagerly for her. "Look at you. All dusty and dirty. You need a good brushing."

The cat lay back in her arms, smugly satisfied with the attention. Tim climbed off the unsteady perch.

"What's that?" Stuffy nodded at the leather roll Tim held in his left hand.

"I don't know. I found it up there between the beams."

Stuffy fingered the edges. "It's buckskin and

very old, I think."

Even Debbie was intrigued enough to forget Bootsie. "Open it, Tim."

He held the long edge and Stuffy helped gently to unroll the stiff leather. In spite of their care it cracked in several places but not badly enough to destroy the markings painted on it. When it was spread open between them, the boys gazed at the signs and symbols. Debbie peered over Stuffy's shoulder.

"What is it?" she asked.

"I don't know," Tim admitted. "It might be a map of some kind, only there aren't any directions or arrows."

"Perhaps . . . but it couldn't be." Stuffy looked around the storage room. "But this house is very old, isn't it?"

Tim sighed, then remembered how Stuffy's silly question about the ceilings had really been important.

"Mr. Perkins said his grandfather built this house."

"I wonder if that is old enough. But the buckskin could be much older."

"What is it?" demanded Debbie. "Or what do you think it is?"

"I may be wrong, but I think perhaps this could be the map leading to the lost treasure of the padres."

A treasure map! Tim's mouth dropped open. Debbie squeezed Bootsie so tightly she yowled in protest and scrambled from her arms. Debbie was so excited she didn't notice Bootsie leave, but Tim shut the door behind the cat. He wasn't going to waste his time coaxing Bootsie out of ceilings when there was treasure to hunt.

5

Clues in the Museum

The map lay on the dusty floor, the corners held down by old horseshoes. Debbie and Tim glanced at it from time to time as Stuffy told them the story of the padres' treasure.

"Yesterday I told Tim how the Spanish padres came to us and we helped them to build the missions. One of them was the Mission of San Raphael."

"That's the one Dad's working on," said Debbie.

Stuffy nodded. "It wasn't on a ranch then. In those days all this country belonged to the Papagos and Pimas. *Alta Pimaria,* the Spaniards called it."

"That means upper Pima country," Tim translated for Debbie.

"I know as much Spanish as you do, Timothy Bowdy. Go on with the story, Stuffy."

"Everything was peaceful except that the Apaches raided now and then. When they did, the people took refuge in the mission. The walls were strong and there was a spring in the courtyard then. Our people and the padres were safe."

"But I thought it was the Apaches who drove the Jesuits away," said Tim.

"No." The Indian boy looked down at his hands and sighed. "Yesterday I told you only that the Indians attacked. I knew you would think I meant the Apaches. I didn't want you to know it was really an uprising of the Pimas and Papagos."

"But Dad said your people were always peaceful."

"Most of the time they were, but there was one named Luis Oacpicagua, who wanted to drive out the Spaniards and rule Pimaria himself."

Tim snorted. "So what are you ashamed of? Ever since Roman days and even before that, I guess, there's always been one man in every country who wanted to rule the world. What makes you think the Papagos were any different? They're just people."

Stuffy brightened. "I'm glad you think so, Tim."

"Besides," added Debbie, "it was a long time ago. Tell us about the treasure."

"Let him tell it his own way. Go on, Stuffy."

"Well, Luis planned the uprising for the end of summer. All the padres were to be killed. Also all the Pima and Papagos who were friendly to the padres. Many of them were," he added proudly.

"How awful," said Debbie. "Slaughtering all those people, I mean."

"It would have been if Luis had succeeded. Missions were attacked from Sonora to the Gila and Colorado rivers, but the padres had been warned. Most of the missions were empty. Only one or two battles were really fought, but they were very bloody. Some of our people fought with Luis. The rest fought beside the padres; sometimes families divided on both sides. The Papagos could fight better than Apaches, when they had to."

"What about San Raphael?" asked Tim. "Was there a battle here?"

"No, one of the altar boys warned the padres. They fled south to safety, but before they left, it is said, they hid a great treasure for the day they'd return."

"But they never did."

"Not to San Raphael. Franciscan padres returned to San Xavier and Tucson, but the little chapel of San Raphael was forgotten. Then the first Mr. Perkins came, and no one bothered with the mission."

"Until now." Debbie smiled dreamily. "I think it's wonderful that Mr. Perkins is restoring it. Just think of all that happening right here."

Tim was more interested in the treasure. "But where does the map fit into the story?"

"It is said that the padres gave a map to the

altar boy who had warned them. They told him if they did not return by spring, the treasure was to be used for our people."

The vision of ironbound chests filled with jewels and pieces of eight faded from Tim's mind. "Then it was found and spent long ago."

"No, it wasn't," said Stuffy. "During the uprising our people fled to the hills of Baboquivari or north to the Pimas along the Gila River. Then, with the Spaniards gone, the Apaches raided more than ever. It was many years before our people returned to their homes near the mission. By then the map had disappeared."

"And now we've found it," said Debbie.

"Maybe," Tim muttered.

"What do you mean, maybe?"

The excitement of finding the map had passed and Tim was beginning to think.

"For one thing," he said, "how did the map get here in the storage room?"

Stuffy shrugged. "Strange things happen in this country. People have lived on this land since the days of the mammoths. Even the Old

Ones had garbage to throw away or treasures to hide. After the summer floods, you can find almost anything along the washes. Old bows, arrowheads, mammoth bones, or perhaps a map. Here in the desert anything is possible."

"Maybe." Tim still wasn't entirely convinced.

Debbie had no doubts. "When do we start looking?"

"You mean where," Tim corrected. "Stuffy, do you recognize anything on this map?"

If it was a map. To Tim it was just an old deerskin with pictures that weren't much better than the ones Debbie had drawn in kindergarten.

Near the top of the deerskin, on one side, was a series of three-sided rectangles, one drawn inside another, with a faded red oblong painted diagonally to it. Stuffy placed a pudgy finger on the drawing and said, "This looks like the walled mountain."

"Where's that?" Tim asked.

"Near Baboquivari, and it's not really walled. It's just a foothill with terraces on three sides.

There are low stone walls around them. The Ho'hokam, the Old Ones, built them, but no one knows why. The fourth side is a cliff. I don't know what that red thing could be."

Below and to the right of that drawing was another one that Debbie identified.

"I know what that is," she said. "It's a saguaro cactus. We saw lots of them driving in from California. It's a saguaro under a rainbow."

Tim snorted. "Who'd put a rainbow on a map?"

"All right, Timothy Bowdy. If you're so smart, what is it?"

"I don't know, but it sure isn't a rainbow." He bent closer to the faded paint and pointed to some tiny marks near Debbie's saguaro. "Are those bushes?"

Stuffy leaned down. "They look like bird tracks."

"Footprints! They're footprints. Look, five steps the way the arm of the saguaro points and two steps down this way." He stared in dismay at Stuffy. "And that's all. They don't lead any-place."

But Stuffy insisted they did. “You don’t have to put the thing or place on the map, because if you are there, you can see it.”

“But where is it?”

“Baboquivari. I am sure of it. Near the terraced hill there is a hole in the rock where Se’ehe pushed evil Ho’ok into the ground. It makes a bridge just like Debbie’s rainbow. That must be the place.”

Tim scratched his head. “And these jagged lines and the Indian designs, what about them?”

“They’re to make the map look pretty,” suggested Debbie.

“Nobody puts things on a treasure map for decoration. But they might draw things to confuse people. Anyway, it’s the only place we can figure out.” He rolled up the deerskin. “Let’s go.”

“How?” asked Stuffy. “It is too far for Chiquita to go in one day.”

“Maybe Mr. Perkins would take us,” said Debbie. “But then we’d have to tell him about the treasure.”

"Well, it's his map, so I guess we'd better tell him anyhow," said Tim.

They found the old rancher crawling around the floor with a yardstick. He didn't give them a chance to explain about the map.

"I'm measuring up for my museum cases," he told them excitedly. "How would you young-'uns like to ride into Tucson with me this afternoon? Want to take a look at the cases in the museum there and get some information. Maybe talk to one of them archaeological fellers."

"I'd like to go," said Debbie.

"But we have something else to do." Tim glared at his sister.

"It is not important," Stuffy said quickly. "We'll be happy to go with you, Mr. Perkins."

They gave Tim no chance to say a word but made arrangements to meet right after lunch. Tim glared and poked them, but Stuffy and Debbie ignored his signals. They didn't stop chattering until they were well away from Mr. Perkins' house.

"What's the idea?" Tim demanded at the first

chance. "Did you two forget all about getting to Baboquivari?"

Debbie pouted. "But I want to go to the museum."

"I think perhaps we should," said Stuffy. "Perhaps somebody at the museum can help us with the map. I am not quite sure we are right. Everything on a map should mean something."

Tim agreed, but he didn't think they should show the map to strangers.

"We can copy the parts we don't know," said Stuffy. "Especially those Indian designs. They look like war shields."

"And I want to go," repeated Debbie. "I want to see something around here besides this awful patio."

They went right after lunch, riding in the back of Mr. Perkins' dilapidated pickup truck. They jounced and jiggled along the dirt road, thrown off their packing-case seats whenever the truck hit a chuckhole. Debbie thought it was fun, though by the time they turned onto the paved highway she declared enough was enough.

They rattled through the center of the city and turned off on the quiet streets leading to the university. Mr. Perkins parked the truck and led them through huge iron gates to the tree-shaded campus. A small white sign identified the first building: Arizona State Museum.

After a small lobby they entered an enormous two-story room. A Navajo rug, larger and finer than any of Mr. Perkins', led to an enormous slice of tree trunk with the growth rings marked off according to historic dates. Here and there, armchairs were grouped around tables piled high with magazines. People were reading, talking in normal voices, or doing homework. It wasn't at all the way Tim thought of a museum. It was more like Mr. Perkins' living room, only bigger and fancier.

"I'm going to do some talking," the rancher told them. "You wander about here and upstairs. Can't get lost nohow. I'll round you up when I'm ready to leave."

For all her fussing about wanting to see the museum, Debbie didn't seem interested in anything but an old one-shoulder Hopi dress. Stuffy was eager to show them the dioramas of the mammoths that had roamed the Papago reservation years ago. Tim finally dragged Debbie away from admiring the bare-shoulder dress, and that turned her ornery. She only glanced at the model of a caveman hacking steaks from a slain mammoth.

"Ugh, how disgusting," she said and pulled the boys away.

She wouldn't let Tim take more than a quick glance at the mummies but pestered to go upstairs. She was even worse up on the balcony. When Stuffy proudly showed them the exhibits of old Papago life, Debbie declared that tattooing the women's chins was horrible.

Tim took one look at Stuffy's face and couldn't bear Debbie's rudeness any longer. How could she stand there and insult Stuffy's ancestors? After all, it wasn't as if they still tattooed.

He stomped off around the balcony into the Mexican section and stood before a photograph of an Aztec temple, fuming inwardly at his sister. If they weren't in a museum, he'd tell her a thing or three.

As he stared at the picture an uncomfortable feeling began nagging at him. The feeling that he'd forgotten something. Something important, but what? He frowned at the stone ruins trying to remember.

Suddenly he shouted, "That's it."

He skidded around a corner, nearly toppling a meteorite from its stand, and ran head on into Stuffy. Tim grabbed the Indian boy and whirled him around.

"I found it, Stuffy. I found the treasure."

"Here?"

"No!" Tim let the boy go and calmed down to explain. "I mean I found out where it is."

"So did I."

"Where? I mean where is what showed you where . . . Oh, I'm so mixed up, I don't know what I mean."

Stuffy laughed. "I know. My clue is in the Papago exhibit. Come look."

"Look at mine first. It's right here."

Tim pointed to the picture. Stuffy looked puzzled, then the wide grin slowly filled his brown face.

"Yes," he said at last. "That will go with what I found. Come see."

They hurried to the Papago display at the head of the stairs. Debbie put down the grinding stones she'd been trying and squeezed in between the boys.

"What's so interesting?" she wanted to know.

The boys ignored her.

"Do you see it?" asked Stuffy.

"No."

"Remember the war shields on the map?"

"Yes, but I don't– Wait! Yes, that proves it."

Stuffy nodded. "But I should have thought of it this morning."

"You would have remembered sooner or later," Tim assured him.

"Remembered what?" Debbie asked. "What are you talking about?"

"The treasure map," they said together.

"Oh, did you ask about those sketches you made?"

"We don't have to ask," said Tim. "Stuffy and I know what they mean."

"How can you if you didn't ask?"

"Because we think." Tim winked at Stuffy. "We know just where to find the treasure."

"Where?"

"Figure it out. It's simple." He turned to the stairs. "Come on, Stuffy. Let's find Mr. Perkins."

"Oh!" Debbie stamped her foot. "I think boys are absolutely disgusting."

Tim grinned. Let her stew until they got home. It served her right for spoiling the museum trip. Though to be honest, if she hadn't made him mad, he might never have gone over to that Aztec exhibit. Of course Stuffy would have recognized the symbols on the map eventually, but the trip had saved them a lot of time and trouble. And it was really because of Debbie that they'd come to the museum. He turned back up the stairs.

"Come here, Debbie. I'll explain it to you."

She tossed her head. "Don't bother."

She flounced past him and plunked herself down in one of the armchairs, refusing even to look at Tim. Being quiet so long must have been a strain because when Mr. Perkins came, she started chattering to the old rancher and didn't stop until he'd boosted her into the back of the truck. Stuffy talked and joked with her on the return trip. By the time Mr. Perkins dropped them at their own patio, Debbie had forgiven Tim for his teasing and was eager to hear about the treasure map.

6

Debbie's Ghost Detector

They sat under the mulberry tree sipping lemonade. Bootsie purred in Debbie's lap. Chiquita's wet nose nudged one shoulder and then another begging for bits of cookie. Tim spread the map carefully on the end of the lounge and pointed to the two designs at the bottom.

"Now, Debbie, you should know what these are."

"How should I know?"

"Because you're the one who raised such a fuss about them." He raised his voice to a squeaky soprano. "It's absolutely horrible to tattoo women's chins," he mimicked.

Debbie stopped petting Bootsie and stared at the deerskin. "You mean these funny things are *women?*"

"Papago women," said Stuffy. "Those little lines on the chins are tattoo marks. You made me think of them."

"And there are two of them," hinted Tim.

Debbie squealed. "Two Sisters."

"And these"—Tim pointed at the three-sided rectangles—"these aren't terraces. They're steps.

A picture of an Aztec temple gave me the idea. Then when Stuffy showed me the tattooed chins, I knew I was right."

Stuffy pushed Chiquita's head aside. "I think perhaps that red block is a bell tower. See how it leans against the steps? That must mean a ruined church with a fallen belfry."

"The Mission of San Raphael." Debbie squeezed Bootsie in her excitement. "Tomorrow we'll have the treasure."

"Right." Tim grabbed a cookie and sprawled back on the lounge.

"Perhaps," said Stuffy.

Tim's hand stopped halfway to his mouth. "What do you mean, perhaps?"

"Well, there is still Debbie's rainbow."

"I thought you said it was a stone arch."

"That was when I thought the treasure was on Baboquivari. There the arch is large enough to ride a horse through. I know of no such arch on Two Sisters."

"Somebody must know. What about your father?"

Stuffy shook his head. "None of my people would know. When the ghost bell was heard, the Old Man of the village said an evil spirit dwelled on Two Sisters. It is said that even the coyotes refused to sing from that peak. No one has gone near it since then, and that was before my grandfather was born."

Tim hunched over the dim markings. The zigzag lines could be steps. Not real steps cut in the hillside but imaginary ones to show the way to the treasure. Yes, that must be it.

"See these lines? I think we must climb the hill from behind the mission, all the way to the base of the twin peaks. From there we can look down through the arch to the saguaro. It must be a small opening that can't be seen from below, or all these lines and the mission wouldn't be needed."

Stuffy grunted as he rose. "I think perhaps I should be going home. My mother expects me before dark."

Tim wanted to talk more about the treasure hunt, but he didn't argue. He knew how it was when his mother told him to be home at a certain time.

"Will you come early tomorrow? It may take all day to climb to the peaks and dig for the treasure."

The boy's face had a closed-up look Tim had never seen before. "Perhaps you shouldn't wait for me. Go on by yourself."

"What's the matter? You aren't afraid of that ghost bell, are you? Not in broad daylight?"

Stuffy twisted Chiquita's reins between his fingers. "Not exactly," he murmured.

"Well, what is it, then?"

"It's just that there are some places where it is better not to go. If people have not gone there for hundreds of years, there must be a good reason."

Tim snorted. Just as he'd thought. Stuffy was afraid of spooks. As if Debbie weren't enough, he'd had to get mixed up with a scarebaby boy. Before he could say anything, Debbie stepped up.

"We want you to come with us, Stuffy."

"Us?" stormed Tim. "Who said you were going?"

"It's as much my treasure as it is yours, Timothy Bowdy. After all, it was my cat that found the map, practically."

Tim rolled his eyes skyward in disgust, but he agreed that Debbie could go with them.

"Thank you." She tossed her head and turned back to Stuffy. "After all you've said, I'm a little scared to go up there myself."

"Then why ask to go?" yelled Tim.

Debbie paid no attention. "But maybe there isn't anything up on Two Sisters now. Maybe whatever it was got tired or sick or just went away."

Stuffy nodded eagerly. He looked at Debbie as if expecting her to produce a magic anti-spook charm.

"You said even coyotes stayed away from Two Sisters," continued Debbie. "Well, I've read lots of ghost stories, and they always say animals can see things people can't. Especially cats. So I'll take Bootsie along, and all we have to do is watch her. If she sees–"

"No!" Tim jumped to his feet. "We're not taking any dumb cat on a treasure hunt."

Debbie jerked him aside and hissed, "Do you want Stuffy to go?"

"Sure, but–"

"No Bootsie, no Stuffy." She nestled the cat under her chin and waited.

Tim knew when he was licked. "All right, you win. We'll take Bootsie with us tomorrow."

"I'll be here early, perhaps," said Stuffy.

He climbed from the lounge onto the mule and rode off looking strange without his usual broad grin.

"I bet that's the last we see of that scare-baby," said Tim.

"Timothy Bowdy, you make me so mad," shouted Debbie. "I hope we *do* find a ghost and I hope it scares you *blue*."

Tucking the cat under her arm she ran into the house. Tim stayed until Chiquita had plodded out of sight across the desert.

The way those two were acting, anybody

would think he'd asked them to go treasure hunting at night. What could happen in bright sunlight? Nothing, worse luck. A treasure hunt should be filled with danger and excitement.

The more he thought of it, the surer Tim was that there was something strange about Two Sisters. Not ghosts, of course, but something unusual. All this superstitious nonsense must have started from something real. But what?

He sighed as he collected the cookie plate and lemonade glasses. No use worrying about it. There wasn't much chance he'd get to the mission at night.

But two hours later they were on their way: Tim, Debbie, and Mr. Bowdy, with that dumb cat perched on top of the blankets. Debbie hadn't been included in Dad's plan, but she'd begged to go along. She'd also insisted on taking Bootsie just in case.

"In case of what?" Dad had asked.

"In case Tim turns blue."

Mr. Bowdy had laughed, but Tim's spine still tingled. All this ghost talk was enough to make anyone nervous.

Mr. Bowdy hunched over the steering wheel, intent on the dirt road. Tim and Debbie were flung from one side to the other as the car swerved around the chuckholes that leaped unexpectedly into the headlights. Even Bootsie had trouble keeping her balance. Twice Tim saw the cat roll off the blankets and claw frantically at Debbie. She didn't even whimper over the scratches on her arm. Why couldn't she be that brave about everything?

The stucco walls of the mission loomed ghostly white against the dark hillside of Two Sisters. A fire in the courtyard guided them to the gate. As soon as they parked beside Mr. Perkins' truck, Tim grabbed blankets and rushed to the firelight.

"Just in time." The rancher pushed hot coals from the lid of a big iron pot. "Supper's ready."

"It smells good."

"Should be. Real chuck-wagon grub."

Tim passed the tin plates and cups. Debbie tried to fork out the steaks and sourdough biscuits, but she couldn't do much with Bootsie dangling under her left arm.

“That critter lost the use of its legs?” asked Mr. Perkins.

“I need her right with me.” She flashed Tim a don’t-you-dare-tell look.

“Then you better set and let me do the dipping.”

They settled around the fire. After everyone had seconds, there was dessert made of raisin dough that tasted a lot better than it looked. Tim enjoyed every mouthful. This was part of what he’d expected to find on the ranch. As he ate he pretended there were cattle bedded down just outside the courtyard. Soon he’d be called for his turn riding herd.

Mr. Perkins called him all right but not to herd cattle.

“You can help Debbie wash the dishes. If it’s any comfort to you, just make out you’re on a cattle drive as cook’s louse.”

“What’s a cook’s louse?”

“Someone who does the dishes.” He grinned and poured more coffee for himself and Mr. Bowdy.

Debbie insisted on drying, so she could keep hold of Bootsie. Tim was surprised how quickly the chore went. In no time at all he was tossing the soapy water into the tumbleweeds and drying the dishpan.

"I reckon you can make out all right in the morning," said Mr. Perkins.

Tim turned in surprise. "Aren't you camping with us?"

"Somebody's got to be in hollering distance of your ma."

"I never thought of that." Debbie should have stayed at home. No, she'd be worse than nothing if another rattler crept onto the patio. He should have stayed. But Dad had asked him to come camping a few nights to prove there was nothing to fear at the mission.

"Don't worry about your mother," said Dad. "She stayed alone many times when I had to travel."

"And I'll be in hearing distance," said Mr. Perkins. "We'll be here before daylight for breakfast."

"We'll have it all ready," Debbie promised.

Mr. Bowdy unrolled the plans he'd drawn for the mission. As the two men discussed them Tim started toward the old building. Sand crunched behind him. He turned to find Debbie at his heels, Bootsie still in her arms.

"Where are you going?" she asked.

"I'm going to listen for the ghost bell."

He'd thought that would send her back to the fire, but she walked on beside him. The flickering flames made the shadows of tumbleweeds grow and shrink on the wall facing them. The rest of the mission was lost in dark lumpy shadows.

"It's spooky," Debbie whispered.

"Want to go back?"

She shook her head. Tim frowned. She should be throwing a scarebaby fit, but she was as calm as he was. He couldn't figure it out.

"You won't hear the bell tonight," she told him.

"How do you know?"

"Look at Bootsie."

So that was the reason she wasn't scared. She was counting on that dumb cat to show her if the spooks were prowling. Bootsie lay in her arms, four paws in the air, eyes half closed.

"We'd better hurry before your ghost detector goes to sleep.

He felt his way through the door and into the church. He'd expected it to be dark, but it wasn't. The roof and back wall were completely gone. So was half of the one side wall. Tim whistled softly. No wonder Dad was willing to try anything to get the workers to camp here during the week. Unless they started working full time soon, they wouldn't finish this summer.

Debbie stumbled into him.

"Watch where you're going," he snapped.

"I can't. I have to watch Bootsie."

A motor coughed and sputtered outside the gate. Then silence.

"Mr. Perkins left. We'd better go back before Dad worries about us."

He reached out a hand to guide Debbie. At

the doorway she stopped him.

"Tim, there's a—a *thing* out there."

"Don't be silly."

"There is," she whispered fiercely. "Look at Bootsie."

The round yellow eyes stared into the darkness outside. As the cat struggled to free itself a hulking blackness moved in the shadows near the wall.

Debbie screamed.

Tim lunged forward in a flying tackle that connected with solid flesh. Whoever it was, he was pretty big because he didn't tumble. Just sat down with a thud with Tim sprawled across the thick legs.

"Got him," Tim yelled.

But he hadn't figured on two of them. Another one jumped on his back and Tim's lungs emptied with a loud grunt.

7

Treasure Hunt

It was like fighting a pair of mattresses, only these had arms and legs. Through the grunts and gasps Tim heard the rancher's cracked voice.

"Hold on, Tim. We're a-coming."

The two prowlers stopped fighting. Flashlight beams crisscrossed on the ground. Tim sat up and fended off a boot kicking wildly in the air.

"Mr. Perkins! What are you doing here?"

"I cooked supper, remember?"

"But I thought you left."

Tim's father bent over him. "Are you all right?"

"Yes, but who's this?" Tim yanked a shirt front, and a round grinning face rose into the beam of light. "Stuffy! What are you doing here?"

"I came with my father."

"And before you ask what he's doing here, I'll tell you," said Mr. Bowdy. "I invited him to camp with us tonight."

As the man beneath him moved Tim caught a glimpse of the emblem on the shirt sleeve: Papago Police. Tim scrambled to his feet. The flashlight showed a king-sized edition of Stuffy, complete with wide grin. Mr. Ramirez puffed as he struggled to his feet and hitched up his levis. Tim found the policeman's hat and brushed it with his sleeve before handing it to the man.

"I'm sorry, Mr. Ramirez. I didn't know it was you."

"He thought you were a ghost," said Debbie.

"I did not. Who ever heard of tackling a ghost?"

After many apologies and a lot of laughter Mr. Perkins drove off in his rickety truck. The truck Tim had heard before belonged to Mr. Ramirez.

Stuffy whispered, "Did Debbie bring the cat?"

"Yes, but don't count on her. She's so dumb she can't tell the difference between a spook and a policeman."

The men were already at the fire. Mr. Bowdy was pouring coffee for Stuffy's father.

"What kind of birds are those?" asked Debbie. "I've never seen any swooping like that at night."

"Those aren't birds," Stuffy said. "They're bats."

With a yelp Debbie charged into camp and grabbed a blanket. She threw it over her head and huddled near the fire.

"What's wrong with her?" asked Mr. Bowdy.

Debbie opened the blanket an inch to answer. "Bats. They'll get in my hair."

When everyone laughed, she peered cautiously through the opening.

"Don't you know bats have built-in radar?" Tim said. "They won't touch you."

"How do you know one of them isn't sick and his radar isn't working? I'll stay under here, thank you."

Stuffy tried to coax her out.

"Let her suffocate," Tim said. "She's just a bat-shy scarebaby."

Debbie had an answer, but it was muffled by the blanket. Tim thought he heard his name and the word blue, but he wasn't sure.

"It's a good thing you brought your daughter," Mr. Ramirez was saying. "The men will be ashamed of themselves when they hear a girl has camped here overnight."

Stuffy glanced over his shoulder and muttered, "I wish Debbie would let that cat out of the blanket, where I could watch her."

His father didn't seem at all nervous. Maybe because he was a policeman, or perhaps grown-ups hid their feelings better. Whatever the reason, Mr. Ramirez rolled up in his blanket as if he'd never heard of any ghost bell. Mr. Bowdy patted the blanket draped over Debbie.

"Time for bed, Debbie."

She held the blanket open like the front of a tent. “Where do we sleep?”

“Just roll up in your blanket and lie down.”

“On the ground? But there are *things* here.”

Mr. Bowdy said sternly, “Deborah, you asked to come on this trip. Now you’ll do exactly as you’re told, with no complaining. Do you understand?”

“Yes, sir.”

Though she didn’t complain aloud, she kept them awake for an hour, moving here and there trying to find a place where *things* couldn’t crawl into her blanket. Tim pulled off his boots and cradled his head on his arms.

He wished he had a saddle for a pillow like a real cowboy, but a least he was camping outdoors. That was more than he’d expected to do three days ago.

For all his nervousness Stuffy was sound asleep already. Only Debbie squirmed and wriggled.

Tim gazed up at the stars, brighter and closer than he’d even seen them. He knew the Big

Dipper right away but couldn't remember how to find the North Star from it. A shooting star flashed toward the horizon and faded. Tim smiled. That was a sure sign they'd find the treasure tomorrow.

Just as he drifted off to sleep Bootsie tried to creep under his blanket. Twice Tim pushed the cat away, but it meowed so pitifully he finally let it curl up behind his knees–on top of the blanket, not under it. He snuggled deeper, wondering how it could get so chilly outdoors at night when the days were so hot.

As usual Debbie caused a commotion in the morning. She refused to move so much as a finger until Dad and Mr. Ramirez had inspected her blanket for *things*. She was sure something crawly had shared her blanket, since Bootsie was nowhere around to protect her. While Tim and Stuffy gathered firewood she wandered around calling the cat.

"I thought you were going to have breakfast ready for Mom and Mr. Perkins?" Tim reminded her.

"I have to find Bootsie. You look for her, Tim."

The tumbleweeds had been cleared from around the mission and camping area, but the round shrubby weeds crowded the rest of the courtyard like huge airy volleyballs. Near the ground the curving branches left triangular spaces where Bootsie could move easily between and around the tumbleweeds, but Tim had no desire to push through the dense thistles. He'd noticed that Debbie, for all her worrying, had only walked around the cleared areas.

"She'll come back. She was gone three days once before."

Mrs. Bowdy drove up with Mr. Perkins and told her the same thing, but the cat hadn't appeared by the time Tim and Stuffy had borrowed a shovel and were ready to climb Two Sisters.

"I'm not going." Debbie's chin quivered. "How can you think of leaving when Bootsie's lost?"

It was Mr. Perkins who headed off the threatening flood of tears.

"That cat found itself a hidey-hole right inside these walls," he told her.

"How do you know?"

"I know critters." The rancher winked at Mrs. Bowdy. "I'm so positive sure, that I'm willing to dig up all these tumbleweeds and move all those loose adobes to prove it. Providing, of course, that cat don't show up in a reasonable length of time."

"What's a reasonable length of time?" asked Debbie.

Mr. Perkins rubbed his chin. "When did you last see that critter."

"Late last night," said Tim. "She tried to crawl in my blanket."

"Timothy Bowdy! You chased Bootsie away."

"I did not." It took a while to convince Debbie it wasn't his fault the dumb cat had disappeared again. "For criminy's sake, you'd think I killed Bootsie, the way you're carrying on."

Stuffy clucked his tongue. "I'm glad I didn't bring Chiquita. I wouldn't want my mule to hear how bad-tempered people are. It might spoil her."

That would have set off another argument about who'd started the fight if Stuffy hadn't picked up the shovel and headed for the hillside. Debbie lingered long enough to get Mr. Perkins' promise to leave no stone or weed unturned if Bootsie didn't appear by noon.

"I'll look, certain sure. Now you go exploring with the boys and enjoy yourself."

"I'll be back at noon to help look for Bootsie," she promised.

"Just like you got breakfast," Tim muttered.

Then he remembered what Stuffy had said about humans being more bad-tempered than mules. From now on he'd be nice to his sister. He honestly tried, but she made it awfully hard. Every rock and bush had to be inspected in case Bootsie had wandered up the hill. She wasted so much time that they weren't halfway to the top when the Papago workers began driving up to the mission. They stopped climbing to rest and watch.

The workers must have left at dawn and it was over an hour since breakfast. If the men left the mission in time to be home by sunset, that would be three hours or more lost each day. It didn't seem like enough to worry about, until Tim realized there were ten to fifteen men down at the mission. His mind rebelled at the arithmetic involved in figuring the weeks or months that would be lost because of a silly superstition.

"I wish I could hear what they're saying," said Debbie.

Stuffy grinned. "They are saying we're all loco for sleeping there last night."

"Will they camp at the mission next week?" asked Tim.

"Perhaps."

"Maybe they won't believe we slept there all night."

"They will believe my father. But to stay there themselves, that is another matter. They may say last night was not the time for the ghost bell to ring."

Debbie looked up from the small cave where she'd been calling Bootsie. "Do you mean we'll have to keep camping here night after night?"

"You weren't scared last night," Tim said.

"I had Bootsie with me."

She and Stuffy exchanged glances. Without Bootsie those two scarebabies wouldn't stay another night. Tim hoped the cat would show up by noon or that Mr. Perkins found her. Otherwise Dad's plan might fall apart. He wondered if Mr. Ramirez had been counting on Debbie's ghost detector too. No, Stuffy's father hadn't even looked at the cat, but he might not stay tonight if Stuffy pleaded to go home. Tim sighed.

Then the men would never camp here and Mr. Bowdy's work wouldn't be finished by the end of August. Then Mr. Perkins wouldn't have his mission opened in time for the winter tourist season, and maybe Dad wouldn't even be paid. Unless Mr. Perkins sold his Indian relics, and that would break his heart. There was so much to worry about, Tim almost forgot what they were doing climbing Two Sisters. He had to stop and think a second when Debbie said, "I don't know why we're going to all this trouble."

"To find the treasure of the padres," puffed Stuffy.

They were almost to the base of the twin peaks that topped the hill.

"I know that," Debbie said. "But the treasure won't belong to us when we do find it."

Tim turned to stare at her, then he remembered. "Of course! It belongs to Mr. Perkins. It's his map and it's on his property. Why didn't I think of that before?"

"You did," Stuffy said. "But then we went to the museum and you forgot about it."

"Why didn't you remind me?"

The chubby shoulders lifted in a shrug. "I didn't think it was important."

"Not important!"

Stuffy sat down on the loose stones to rest and explain. "I don't think Mr. Perkins would want the treasure. It isn't money he wants."

"Then what does he want?"

"I know," exclaimed Debbie. "He wants people."

Stuffy nodded.

"Don't you see, Tim? Mr. Perkins is lonely. That's why he's opening the museum and the mission. Remember how he told us that people would come out every day? And how he wants to open the coffee shop, so they won't hurry right off but stay and talk?"

"And my mother is to run the coffee shop," said Stuffy proudly.

Tim remembered how glad Mr. Perkins always was to see him at the door. And how the rancher had spent a whole morning showing him how to skin a rattler. Stuffy was right. The old rancher was lonely.

He glanced at the crumbling walls far below. San Xavier and Tumacacori were famous missions and easier to reach. Who'd come out here to San Raphael? It was too small and unimportant. No one would bother driving out here unless there was something really different about San Raphael.

Tim hauled Stuffy to his feet. "Come on. We've got to find that treasure. Not just for ourselves but for Mr. Perkins."

"But Stuffy said he wouldn't want it," protested Debbie.

"Maybe he doesn't want jewels and gold, but just think how many people will come out here to see where the Spanish treasure was found. Why, more people will come to see that than the mission."

"Tim is right," said Stuffy.

Debbie sighed and stood up. "All right, let's get on with it."

Tim drew the map from its hiding place inside his shirt. They stood at the base of the rocky peaks. Directly below them was the mission.

"This way," said Tim. He led them around the base of the peaks. "There!"

A short way down to their right was the stone arch. It was only chest high, but by squatting on their heels they could see a long slope of hillside through it.

"Oh, no," groaned Tim. "Now what do we do?"

On the map in Tim's hand a saguaro pointed the way to the treasure. There were dozens of saguaros growing on Two Sisters, but none of them could be seen through the arch.

8

Beneath Two Sisters

"We should have thought of that before," said Tim. "Plants don't live forever."

Debbie smirked. "I seem to remember someone saying that he *always* took time to think."

Tim squared off for an argument, but Stuffy said loudly, "Ribs."

Stuffy's other far-off remarks had turned out to be important, but no matter how Tim twisted and turned the word ribs, he could make nothing of it.

"I give up," he said. "What about ribs?"

"They last."

Tim scratched his head. "I guess they do. At

least they do if you don't crack one playing football or falling off a horse."

"I mean saguaro ribs. The saguaro lives a hundred years or more. When it dies, the ribs are left on the ground. Those sticks on your porch ceiling are saguaro ribs. They were put up when the house was built and they're still there."

Then the remains of the saguaro painted on the map might still be lying down there on the hillside. But if this was the map of the padres' treasure, wouldn't it be too old for even saguaro ribs to be left? No, he wouldn't begin doubting now. Not when they were almost at the end of the trail.

Since Stuffy knew what to look for, Tim and Debbie sat down to watch him through the small stone arch. Now and then Tim called directions to keep him on course.

"Tim," said Debbie. "What happened to the mission? I can't see it even when I stand up."

Tim snorted. "Of course not. We walked around the peaks, remember? If we go straight down the hill from here, we'll be about a third of the way around the hill from the mission. This mountain's like a cone– Look!"

Stuffy waved both arms in the air. "I found it," he yelled. "Which way do I walk?"

The arm on the saguaro cactus showed clearly enough on the map. Tim gestured. Together he and Debbie peered through the arch and counted the steps. One, two, three, four, five.

"Now two steps this way," Tim called. "No, turn around more. That's it."

One . . . and Stuffy disappeared from view. They tumbled and slid down the hill, Tim dragging the shovel behind him. Stuffy stood before a hollow, staring at a patch of sand caught between two rocky outcroppings.

"Perhaps we don't need the shovel," he told Tim.

"Why not? Isn't this the place?"

"Yes, I'm sure of it, but perhaps you can dig deep enough with your hands."

"Not me." Stubbornly Tim stomped the shovel into the sand. Stuffy lowered himself to a flat boulder and watched silently. On the third shovelful the sand turned color. By the fifth it was definitely wet. Tim wiped his face and leaned on the handle. Silently they watched the hole he'd dug slowly fill with water.

"How do we get the treasure with all that water in the way?" asked Debbie.

"That water is the treasure," answered Stuffy.

"It can't be."

"Not now. Not to you. But perhaps if someone had been traveling many days from Tucson, leading a burro, and had found no water, perhaps then this bit of water would be more precious than gold."

"But I'm not a prospector," insisted Debbie. "And I don't need this mud puddle to save my life."

"But water is the greatest treasure of all."

"Not to a drowning man."

"Oh, for criminy's sake," groaned Tim. "There she goes again."

"To a drowning man in the middle of the ocean," continued Debbie, "a bit of desert would be a treasure more precious than gold."

Stuffy's eyes twinkled. "Until he had been on that desert a while. Then his treasure would be fresh water."

"Oh, you have water on the brain," snapped Debbie. "There's no sense trying to talk to you."

Tim grinned as she stalked to a boulder and perched on it with her back to the boys.

"That's the first time anyone ever argued her down. If I had a canteen, Stuffy, I'd give you my share of the treasure for that." Tim sobered. "Did you mean what you said? That this spring is really the treasure?"

"The treasure for this map but not the treasure of the padres." Stuffy picked up the map and spread it over his crossed legs. "When I saw where the map led, I began to think. I thought how strange it is that all the symbols on the map are Indian symbols."

"That's true," said Tim. "But if the priests drew it for Indians to follow, wouldn't they have used Indian symbols?"

"Perhaps, but why should the priests bother with this little spring? There was a much better one inside the courtyard."

"What happened to it?"

Stuffy shrugged. "Some say it was taken as punishment to the people for the uprising. The old songs say that evil Ho'ok stole it so the priests could never return to San Raphael."

"Isn't that Ho'ok the one that's supposed to be underground?"

Stuffy nodded.

"Then the songs are probably just a fancy way of saying there was an earthquake."

"Perhaps. The songs say the evil one laughed afterward. That could mean the earth shook."

"And that's how all the nonsense about Two Sisters began."

"Perhaps, but it does not explain the ringing of the ghost bell. That was heard many times and there was no ground shaking then."

Debbie spun around on her boulder. "But what about the map? If it isn't the altar boy's, whose is it?"

"If you just think about it, you'll know," said Tim. "The uprising is over. The priests have gone. So has the spring. Now who needs water?"

"My people," said Stuffy. Then he looked puzzled. "But what would my people need with a map?"

"To show Mr. Perkins' grandfather where to find water when he used the courtyard for branding. One of your ancestors must have drawn it for him. When he no longer needed it, he shoved it up in the beams." He rubbed his shirt sleeve over his forehead. "Now, how about sampling some of Stuffy's desert treasure?"

They took turns kneeling to drink. Debbie squealed when the water went up her nose. Stuffy laughed.

"It is a wonder all the Indians didn't drown drinking this way," he said. "Or perhaps that is the reason they learned to make pots."

"All this trouble for nothing," grumbled Debbie. She inspected the ground carefully before sitting beside the Indian boy. "I thought surely we'd find something wonderful with that map."

Tim agreed, though he remembered that he'd had doubts. Then he'd been caught up in the excitement of the search. It had been fun. Too bad it was over. Or was it?

The treasure was still here someplace. In their

haste to leave, the padres couldn't have carried it too far from the mission. Surely he and Stuffy could figure out the location if they just set their minds to it. There weren't many places to hide a treasure out here.

He looked for some shade, but the sun was overhead. Only a narrow band of shadow ran diagonally down the hill along the rocky ledge. It was noon. Tim wondered if Bootsie had returned or if Mr. Perkins was hacking away at the tumbleweeds in this hot sun.

Tim's eyes stared longingly at the band of shade running down the hill. Here and there the sun lit a section of the ridge, and the rock strata clearly showed layer after layer of various types of rock that had been deposited on the earth and then either eroded or thrust up so that the yellow, brown, and reddish bands were a clearly visible history of the earth's development. Tim wondered if the Indians called them Ho'ok's blankets. It was easy to imagine some mythical monster stretching and pushing them upward. And there was even a place where the monster had gotten his feet tangled.

Tim sat up and squinted at the ridge. Only in that one spot were the waving tinted bands interrupted, as if a slide had fallen over the ridge. No, not exactly like a slide either, for the rocks didn't look the right color.

"Debbie, how many little caves did you look in today while we were climbing?"

"Dozens, I guess." She clapped her hand to her forehead. "Oh, I forgot all about Bootsie."

"Well, forget her again. This is important." For once she listened. "Now those were all little caves, but there could be a big one here on Two Sisters, couldn't there?"

Stuffy looked doubtful. "Perhaps, but I have never heard of one."

"But nobody's been up here since the uprising, or soon after. You said so yourself. Just suppose there is a big cave. And suppose the old priests hid the treasure in it."

"All right," said Debbie. "We're supposing."

"Well, how close to the mission would you say the cave would have to be? I mean, is this too far away for them to have carried the treasure?"

They were both staring at him, tense with excitement.

"Well," he prompted. "How far?"

"It depends on the treasure," said Stuffy.

"If it was water they hid—" Debbie began, but Tim's glare stopped her.

"Look down there. Do you notice anything funny about that ledge? Look at the shadows."

Stuffy sat up and squinted into the sunlight.

"Look at what?" asked Debbie. "What is it?"

"The water has washed over the ridge for many years," explained Stuffy. "Do you see how it has cut away the loose rock? The shadows go up and down in the ridges."

"Yes, I see that."

"Down there the shadows are lumpy, not at all like the rest."

"And there's the rock strata," Tim said. "See how the layers are one on top of the other all along the ridge?"

Debbie jumped to her feet. "And in the lumpy shadows there aren't any layers. It's all jumbled."

Tim nodded. “As if someone closed up a cave.”

“Perhaps,” said Stuffy. “It may just be a slide.”

“But it’s worth looking at.”

Even Debbie agreed. As they drew closer to the spot the difference in shadow was less noticeable, and the rains had washed so much dirt over the ridge that Tim wondered if it wasn’t just another outcropping instead of a man-made wall. They climbed up and around the mound. Debbie complained about missing lunch and worried aloud about her cat. Tim was ready to call it quits when Stuffy let out a whoop. He’d found an opening large enough to put his head through.

“And look at this.” He pulled something from a jagged rock. Tim and Debbie bumped heads trying to see what he held between his fingers.

“Bootsie’s fur,” cried Debbie.

Stuffy rolled the fine black hairs between thumb and finger. “Perhaps skunk.”

“How would that dumb cat get way over

here?" asked Tim.

"They're Bootsie's. I just know it."

Tim signaled Stuffy not to argue. If this was a cave, only the hope of finding Bootsie would get Debbie inside it. He grabbed the side of the opening and pulled. A large rock broke away in a shower of dirt and shale.

"It *is* a cave," Debbie shouted.

Even Stuffy's eyes sparkled with excitement as he helped pull away another rock.

"We'll need a flashlight," Tim said.

"I'll go get one," said Debbie.

Tim frowned. If Bootsie had been found at the mission, Debbie might not come back. Stuffy knew the way, but he didn't know where Dad kept the flashlight in the car. Tim could go himself, but that would leave Stuffy to open the cave by himself. Debbie wouldn't be much help.

"All right," he told her. "But be sure to come back."

Stuffy told her not to walk around the hill. "You might get lost in the gulleys and outcroppings. Better to climb back up and walk around the peak until you see the mission."

"And come back, no matter what," Tim warned her.

She returned sooner than he'd expected, panting and urging them to hurry.

"Bootsie hasn't come back and Mr. Perkins is chopping weeds all over the courtyard. I just know Bootsie's in this cave. Hurry, Tim."

She placed the flashlight carefully out of the way of falling stones and began clawing at the dirt-packed rocks.

"I suppose they have already eaten at the mission," said Stuffy wistfully.

"Oh, I forgot." Debbie fished a handful of crushed cookies from her pocket. "It's all I could manage without having to answer a lot of questions."

"You didn't tell them about the cave?" asked Tim.

"Of course not."

They worked more than an hour. Their faces became streaked with dirt and sweat. Their fingernails broke painfully. But at last the opening was large enough for them to enter slightly stooped. Tim checked to see there were no loose rocks overhead to fall and block the opening. Then the three of them stepped back and looked uncertainly at one another. Someone had to go first.

Tim picked up the flashlight and led the way.

Twisted rock formations cast weird shadows as the beam of light played over them. An old root looked like a small lizard. Tim touched it gingerly and whistled softly. It was petrified. This cave was much older than the treasure map.

"This dust is terrible," said Debbie behind him. "I feel as if I'm eating mouthfuls of dirt."

"Perhaps this will help." Stuffy gave her the red bandanna he wore knotted around his neck.

Debbie tied it like a bandit mask and nodded. "Thanks, it is better."

They needed more than one flashlight. Tim had to find a way around spires and holes, then turn and light the way for Debbie and Stuffy. It took a long time, especially when they came to a short tunnel where they had to travel through one at a time.

Debbie complained of the chill. Tim wondered how they'd manage if one of them sprained

an ankle or something. Maybe Debbie should have told Mom where they were going. Better yet, they should have waited until Dad or Mr. Perkins could come along. What if another earthquake trapped them inside the mountain? No one would ever find them.

He leaned against a rippled stone column and watched Debbie's sneakers and then Stuffy's worn boots stumble toward him. He'd never felt this way before, not even on the first trip up to the high diving board. Then he'd just been nervous. This was more than that. More than just thinking of all the real things that could happen. His scalp tingled and his shoulders could feel the weight of tons and tons of dirt and rock piled over him. It wasn't the dust that made it difficult for him to breathe or the cave chill alone that made him shiver.

Debbie gave him a push. "Go on, Tim. What are you waiting for?"

He sighed and moved on. He was probably worrying for nothing. Debbie wasn't afraid. Neither was Stuffy. So what was he getting nervous about? But the farther they went into the hill, the more jittery he became. He was actually glad to find the floor of the cave drop away in a sheer cliff.

"End of the line," he said. "There's no way down this."

He felt Debbie shudder as the light flickered over the jagged rocks thirty feet below.

"Bootsie wouldn't fall, would she?" She called the cat, but only the echo of her own voice answered.

"Stop that," Tim snapped. Then to cover his show of fright he added, "You'll wake the bats."

She clapped her hand over the bandanna. The dust in it made her sneeze. Idly Tim directed the beam of light along the bottom of the gorge and then up the sheer wall opposite.

"What was that?" asked Stuffy. "Back a little. There."

Across the gorge, to their right and a little above them, was the dark opening of another cave. On the stones around it were strange marks, man-made marks.

"There must be a way over," said Debbie. "Someone painted those."

"Indians," guessed Tim. "They probably had ladders or one of those swinging rope bridges."

He wiped his forehead. Much as he wanted to go back, he wasn't going to be the one to suggest it. Nobody was going to call him a scarebaby. He wasn't scared, just tired of feeling the weight of Two Sisters pressing on his shoulders. In spite of himself he shuddered.

Stuffy had crept away on hands and knees. Now he called Tim to bring the light.

"In that tunnel back there I noticed how smooth the floor was," he explained. "Almost as if it had been a trail. Here again it feels smooth."

Not only was it smooth, the outer edge was rimmed with small rocks. The path narrowed to fit a ledge that ran along the cliff and around the end of the gorge. The deepest end, Tim noticed. And the small edging rocks wouldn't keep anyone from falling.

From where they crouched, there was no way

of knowing if the ledge widened in front of the cave or even if it reached the opening. They might creep along only to find the ledge broken off or narrowing to nothing. But a path meant people had once come often to this cave–Indians who painted the walls and perhaps Jesuit priests with load after load of treasure.

For a moment Tim's nervousness vanished. Then he remembered the dark opening of the cave across the gorge. Here at least there was room to move and breathe. Who knew what they'd find in there or what might happen crossing the ledge? But the decision wasn't up to him. He raised the flashlight and looked at their faces.

"Well?" he said.

9

Tim Turns Blue

After a moment of lip chewing, Debbie's face settled determinedly.

"I'll go if Stuffy does."

The Indian boy looked as worried as Tim felt, but he nodded.

"All right," said Tim. "Who goes first?"

"You," they said together.

"Thanks," he answered bitterly, but it turned out that he had the best of it.

A surefooted Indian would probably have walked swiftly along the path with his torch. Tim had run atop patio walls a lot narrower, but they were only five feet high and soft grass would have cushioned his fall. It was different knowing the blackness covered a house-high fall to jagged boulders.

His boots felt large and clumsy. He wished he'd taken them off, but then he'd have had no way to carry them. He edged along close to the cave wall and tried to put everything from his mind except the small spotlight at his feet. When the ledge began to curve around the end of the gorge, he flattened himself against the wall and turned the light back.

"If I go any farther, I may not be able to light your way from around the curve," he called. "Come one at a time and keep your eyes on the light at your feet."

Debbie came first, crawling on her hands and knees. With the red bandanna over her face she looked like a cowardly outlaw sneaking away from the vigilantes. When she was safely at Tim's feet, he sent the beacon back to guide Stuffy. The boy eased his bulk along sideways, his back against the wall.

"Now don't move a finger until I get over," Tim warned.

Debbie gasped. "You aren't going to leave us in the dark?"

"I have to. It's the only safe way. Now don't move."

The ledge wasn't dangerous as long as they were still, but any careless movement in the darkness might topple them into the gorge. Tim hurried. Luckily the ledge soon widened to a shelf five or six feet deep. Quickly Tim lit the way for Debbie and Stuffy. They were both shaking when they reached his side.

"And to think we have to go back the same way," Debbie wailed.

"You should have thought of that before we crossed," said Tim.

Stuffy patted her arm. "It will be easier going back."

"Why? It won't be any wider or lighter."

"But we will be on our way out. That makes a difference."

Silently Tim agreed, but as long as they were here they might as well look around. He moved forward and flashed the light over the strange markings. They had been carved into the rock before they were painted. No writing Tim had ever seen looked like that, nor were they pictures.

"Do you know what they mean, Stuffy?"

"No, but I have seen marks like them."

"Where?"

"Here and there in the canyons. The men from the museum call them petroglyphs, but they are really the magic of the Ho'hokam, the Old Ones."

It was useless to ask what kind of magic. Stuffy was as unreasonable about the Old Ones as Debbie was about Bootsie. Even now he looked around as if expecting a spook to jump out of the rock.

Scarebaby, Tim thought scornfully. He ducked into the opening. It was a tunnel higher than the other they'd come through. At first he walked crouched over, the flashlight down and slightly back to give light to Debbie and Stuffy as they crept after him.

The tunnel seemed endless. A rock scraped

his back. He fell to his knees and crawled forward. The tunnel narrowed, catching first one sleeve then the other. Two Sisters was squeezing him. He'd be crushed. Frantically he pushed back.

Debbie yelped. "Timothy Bowdy, take your dirty boots out of my face."

That dumb Debbie! The mountain was burying him alive and all she could do was yell and push him from behind. His angry sob turned to a strangled choke as his mouth filled with dust and a foul smell. Stones cut his hands and bruised his knees through the levis, but suddenly the tunnel walls opened and set him free.

Chest heaving, Tim stood up. Debbie pushed against his legs. He moved forward to give her and Stuffy room to pass. To hide his shaking hands he kept the light dancing around the cave. In one corner rubbish and broken pots were heaped higher than Tim's head. Around the walls were more of the petroglyphs. On ledges stood huge baskets and bowls like the broken ones they'd seen in the museum. But what Tim noticed most was the size. The cave wasn't much larger than Mr. Perkins' storage room, and the rubbish pile took up nearly half. Again he felt the mountain closing in. Sweat broke out in spite of the chill.

"What a horrible smell," said Debbie.

"That's from the bats," Stuffy told her. "A small cave and lots of bats."

"Then I'd better put the kerchief over my head."

Tim tried to concentrate on their talk instead of his weak knees. Already he could feel the walls of the cave closing in, pressing against him.

"Tim," Stuffy called. "Come over to this wall. It feels funny."

Scarebaby Stuffy was groping around in the dark while Tim did nothing but order his knees to stiffen. A fine way for him to feel, but he couldn't shake the strange weakness and growing dread.

Debbie bumped against him. Her arm knocked his hat off.

"Watch out." He was almost screaming.

"What are you doing?"

"I'm waving my arms to keep the bats away from my head."

"Oh, for criminy's sake."

She shuffled into him again, jostling his arm. The circle of light flew across the cave roof illuminating dozens of small black creatures hung upside down. One spread its wings and squeaked.

Debbie screamed at the top of her lungs and plunged headlong for the tunnel.

"Stop," Tim yelled. "Don't run out there."

He grabbed for his sister and then froze as rocks thumped and rumbled overhead. The bats squeaked and filled the small cave with their flittering. Debbie screamed again, put both hands on Tim's chest, and shoved. He fell backward against the jagged wall. With a tinkle of glass the flashlight went out.

The noise of falling rock lasted no longer than Tim could hold his breath. Earthquake, he thought but that was all he could think. His mind was frozen as stiff as his body. He clung

helplessly to the rocks, his mouth open as he heaved great rasping breaths of the dusty stale air.

They were trapped. Even if the mountain hadn't caved in, there was no way out without the light. They could never manage that ridge in the dark. They'd be here forever. Something he'd never felt before welled up from the soles of his feet until he could taste it in the back of his throat. Fear! For the first time he could remember, Tim was too afraid to think.

He wanted to beat against the rock, but even in the midst of his terror he knew clawing at the cave walls would not free him. He slid down and sat limply on the rubbish heap. Two trembling bodies pressed close to him. Someone's teeth chattered. His? Surely he was too scared even for that.

"Tim," sobbed Debbie. "What are we going to do?"

He tried to swallow the bitter taste and couldn't. Debbie shook his arm.

"Tim, think of something."

He thought. He thought of Mom and Dad. How long before they'd begin to worry? Would they ever know what had happened? Maybe one of the Papagos could follow their trail from the mission. He felt easier until he remembered that trailing was an old art. It was probably as lost as the meanings of the petroglyphs.

"I think he's hurt," Debbie was saying. "Maybe a bat bit him."

"Bats don't bite," Stuffy answered. "A rock, perhaps, on his head."

Hands ruffled his hair. If his mouth wasn't so dry, he'd laugh. Those two scarebabies feeling for broken bones and he, Timothy Bowdy, scared stiff. Or was it blue?

He bet he'd turned color just the way Debbie had wished. He reached his hand toward the dim light but it was too high and faint to see more than one bit of the roof. If only it were lower where it would do some good.

Light? There couldn't be light. Tim blinked, but the pale whiteness still lay on the rocks high above him so weak and faint that they hadn't been able to see it with the glare of the flash-light.

"Look," he shouted. "There's an opening up there. It must be where the bats go in and out."

"That's the wall I wanted to show you," said Stuffy. "It feels strange."

"Well, we can't look at it now. Not since scare–" Tim turned but couldn't see his sister's face in the dark. Bats were nothing to be afraid of, but if Debbie felt the way he had just now, maybe she couldn't help the way she acted. "Not since the flashlight broke," he finished.

He ignored the funny noise from Debbie's direction.

"What did the wall feel like, Stuffy?"

"I may be wrong, but it felt like those big adobe bricks on the mission."

Tim crawled over the rubbish, one hand groping blindly before him, until his fingers touched a rough surface. With both hands he traced rough ridges and the smoother rectangles they bordered.

"It's brick all right. But who'd want to brick up a cave?"

"Someone who wished to hide something," said Stuffy.

"There's nothing in here but old jars and pots. Of course if they're from the Old Ones, they might be valuable." Still, that wouldn't be any reason to wall off the cave.

He felt the wall again, wondering if what he thought was possible.

"If only we had a light." He sighed.

"I'm sorry," Debbie said in a small voice.

Tim didn't say it was all right, because it wasn't. They needed that flashlight. Without it that bit of light on the ceiling was their only hope of escape. But if his guess was right, it was sure to lead them to safety.

"Do you realize where we are?" Tim asked. "We must be right underneath the mission."

"That's silly," said Debbie.

"No, it isn't. We twisted and turned so much in that cave, we could be anyplace. Why not under the mission? If this wall is really made of the same bricks as San Raphael, then the priests must have had it built. They wouldn't have gone to all that trouble just to hide a few Indian relics, so this wall must be part of the mission. The foundation or whatever."

Debbie giggled.

"What's so funny?"

"Can you just imagine what's happening up there? I must have scared them out of their wits when I screamed."

Tim stared in the direction of her voice. Of course, that was what caused the rumbling that had scared him so badly. Debbie's shrill scream echoing across the top of the cave had carried into the mission. The workers had probably dropped whatever bricks and rocks they'd been carrying and fled. He groaned.

"To think there's help right over our heads and no way to let them know we're here."

"We can yell," suggested Debbie.

"You've done enough yelling. I doubt if there's anyone up there now to hear us."

Stuffy agreed. "They will be standing in the courtyard to see what will happen next."

"If we keep quiet, maybe they'll go back inside," said Debbie.

"No, if nothing happens, they will just go away."

"And not come back," added Tim. "We have to get out by ourselves."

He pulled off his boots and crawled up the sliding pile of rubbish. When he stood at the top, the roof of the cave was still a foot above his fingertips and the opening just beyond his reach to the right. With his left hand he felt along the natural cave wall for foot and hand holds. He was soon high enough to stretch across the brick wall to the opening.

"Hand me the flashlight," he ordered.

"But it's broken," said Debbie.

"I want it anyway."

The rubbish pile rattled as she climbed toward him. He groped until he felt the metal case heavy with batteries. With the end he pounded the wall next to the opening. It was hard, slow work, stretched out the way he was, but at last he had one brick pounded loose.

"Stand back," he warned. "I'll throw it down. We can use the pieces for hammers."

He loosened two more before his arms began to shake with the strain. He climbed down to let Stuffy take his place. The boy hesitated.

"Did you see over the wall?" he asked at last.

Tim shook his head, then realized Stuffy couldn't see him. "No, why?"

"Nothing."

"It must be something."

"Only a little thing perhaps. But when adobe dries in the sun for many years it gets very hard."

"And?"

"I said it was just a little thing."

Tim frowned as Stuffy climbed up to hammer at the wall. As more bricks came away he understood what Stuffy meant. Though the hole grew larger the light remained dim. It brightened enough to make the bats stir uneasily and shift roosts to darker corners but not anything like it should be if they were working their way outside.

He said nothing aloud. Debbie had enough to worry about with the restless bats. He took a half brick from Stuffy and wearily climbed up for his turn. He forced himself to loosen one brick before he looked. The hole was much wider but not low enough yet for him to put his head through. He could only see up, but as far as he could see there was only the shadowy roof of another cave. Angrily he shoved the brick right through the opening, listening with satisfaction as it crashed and broke somewhere below.

Then it began. A small wailing siren that stirred the hair on Tim's neck. No one moved, not even a bat. There was no sound but the thin howl, rising, falling, then fading away.

Tim gulped. Beyond the wall was another cave and something live was in it.

10

The Altar Boy's Map

Tim climbed down as quietly as possible. Debbie clutched his arm so tightly her finger-nails hurt.

"What is it?" she whispered.

"I couldn't see." Tim was annoyed with him-self for whispering back. None of them seemed willing to raise their voices for fear of disturbing whatever lurked beyond the wall.

"Look," he went on, "let's think this over sensibly. We can't go back over the ledge with-out a light. Our only chance is over this wall."

"But the *thing*."

"It can't climb this wall. At least I don't think

it can. We'll make the hole larger so we can see what it is."

His sister's hand trembled. "I don't think I want to."

"Then Stuffy and I will look at it. We'll throw bricks at it and chase it away. If it got in, it can certainly get out again." And maybe they could too. For the first time Tim was sure they'd get out from under Two Sisters.

"Maybe it doesn't want to go away," Debbie said. "Maybe it will attack."

Scarebaby was at the tip of his tongue, but Tim held it back. He pulled himself back up the wall. At the first blow the yowl rose again. Stuffy's chuckle came from the darkness below.

"What's so funny?" snapped Tim.

"I have been thinking what kind of animal would make such a noise. An angry jaguar perhaps, but they are very rare here. Also, it isn't loud enough for so large an animal. Still, I think it is the voice of a cat. A very angry or frightened cat."

Hands tugged Tim's pantleg. "Timothy

Bowdy, you get down from there and let me up. That's Bootsie."

"I never heard Bootsie make a noise like that."

"Stuffy said it was a little cat. A frightened one. It *must* be Bootsie and you're scaring her blue."

"Bootsie," Tim called toward the opening. "Kitty, kitty Bootsie."

Silence, then a loud meow answered him.

"I knew it," Debbie shouted. "I knew she was in this cave."

Tim slid down and handed Debbie the brick.

"Use some of that energy where it'll do some good. After all, it's your cat."

There went his hope of getting out. That cat could crawl between ceiling beams. Bootsie might get out the way she'd gotten in, but that didn't mean they'd be able to follow her.

Stuffy took a turn at the wall. The opening was much wider and easier to reach. The work went faster. By the time Tim finished his turn he was able to pull himself over the wall into the second cave. This one was lighter and the air fresher, but in his first quick glance before helping Debbie he saw no way out. Three more bricks had to be removed before Stuffy wriggled through. Even then it was a tight squeeze.

A dusty, scrawny Bootsie rubbed against Debbie's ankles.

"At least someone's happy," said Tim.

They slumped to the floor too exhausted to explore their new prison. Tim waited for the fear of the mountain to return. It came but not as strong as before, probably because of the fresher air and the half light.

He could see now that there were not two caves but one large one divided by the adobe wall. Why anyone should take the trouble still puzzled Tim.

Debbie scolded Bootsie gently. "How did you get in here?"

"Perhaps she came the same way as the bats," said Stuffy.

"I thought the bats came in the same way we did," said Tim.

The boy shook his head. "That is too far. They must come in here, but this half of the cave is too light, so they found the opening into the dark half. Perhaps this morning the cat saw them returning and followed."

"And couldn't get out again," finished Debbie. "Poor Bootsie."

Tim pushed himself up and went to look at the source of the pale light. He groaned. High up was the tantalizing sight of the single thick stem of a tumbleweed with the fine leafless branches curving out and up beyond his vision. But the opening that gave him this glimpse of the outside world was too small for anyone except Bootsie to crawl through.

Stuffy limped up beside him. "Perhaps we could tie a message to the cat's neck."

"That dumb cat would probably eat it or lose her way." But Bootsie could certainly have gotten out if she'd wanted to. The cave wall wasn't that steep. Why hadn't she answered Debbie's calls this morning? Tim shrugged. Too dumb, that's why.

"The hole could be dug out," Stuffy said.

Tim nodded. "If we had something to dig with."

He thought of the shovel left way back at the other end of the cave. Even if they had it, he doubted he could lift one shovelful. He'd never been so tired or hungry before.

Stuffy hiked up his levis and grinned. "If we don't soon get out, my clothes will be too big."

"Let's find something to dig with."

If Stuffy was willing to try, so was he. On this side of the wall the cave was long and narrow. Tim walked into the darker end and blinked.

"Stuffy, look at this."

Huge baskets and jars lined the cave wall, row after row, on ledges chipped from the rock. Not ornate black decorated jars, like the ones in the other half of the cave, but the common red clay ollas he'd found in the storage room. The baskets too were finely woven but undecorated.

"Water jars and storage baskets," shouted Stuffy. He peered into one basket after another. "Empty. The pack rats and mice have carried away everything but this." He held out three red grains of corn.

"And that." Tim picked up a stone and heaved it at a dark shape at the very end of the cave. The loud peal of a bell filled the cave and deafened them.

"The ghost bell." Debbie pushed between the boys to see. Bootsie struggled from her arms and hid among the storage baskets.

"The priests hung it from the ceiling," Tim said. "The mice must have run along those upper ledges and knocked bits of stone over the edge."

He dropped a smaller stone onto the rim of the bell. The ring was clear but not so loud.

"The sound echoes in the cave and carries upward, like Debbie's screams. And that, my friends, is how you make a ghost bell."

Debbie sighed heavily. "Poor Dad. How will he ever get it out over that ledge?"

Tim was about to ask why she thought Dad would ever know about the bell, but changed his mind. A scarebaby fit wouldn't help any.

"I don't think the priests brought it in that way. There must be an opening from this cave into the mission."

"Then there's a way out."

"But not that way," said Stuffy. "The whole floor of the mission is covered by the ruins of the belfry."

Debbie's eyes widened. Her chin quivered.

"Stop that," snapped Tim. "We'll get out."

"How?"

"We'll think of something." But what?

He walked over to stare again at the bit of tumbleweed visible through the hole. Mr. Perkins had said he'd clear the whole courtyard to look for Bootsie. Was he still working up there? He seemed like the kind of person who'd do exactly what he promised. He certainly hadn't found Bootsie, and there were still tumbleweeds around the hole.

They could yell from here, but with all those big weeds the hole might never be found. If only they had something that could be seen. A flag of some kind.

"Debbie, give me that bandanna on your head."

"What for?"

"I'll show you, if we can find a stick or a pole." There wasn't any. Tim sighed. "We need something to push this kerchief up through that tumbleweed so it can be seen."

Stuffy picked up one of the water jars and banged it against the rocks. It shattered into small pieces, but the second one he broke left a wedge two feet long and narrow enough to go through the opening, after they'd trimmed it here and there. With trembling fingers Tim tied the red handkerchief to the jagged point.

"Let's hope it holds and that I can reach far enough."

With a helping boost from Stuffy he pulled himself once more up the side of the cave. If he ever got out of here, he'd never look at another rock as long as he lived.

Carefully he maneuvered the chunk of pottery through the opening. The makeshift flag caught on the thorns of the tumbleweed. Tim pulled

gently, praying the knot would hold. It did. But he couldn't climb high enough to get more than his forearm above the ground. The bandanna didn't wave but just rested on top of the weed. It might be enough if someone heard them and began searching.

"Now yell," he ordered, and hoped the workers were still wandering around the courtyard to hear them.

Three voices lifted in a chorus of yells, screams, screeches, and whistles while Tim tried his best to wave the awkward flag. His parched throat grew hoarse. His arm ached unbearably; the muscles twitched. He couldn't hold it another second.

Steel glinted at the base of the tumbleweed. The weed vanished with a swish and Mr. Perkins' weathered face peered down.

"Never heard such caterwauling in my life. Worse than a bunch of fresh-branded calves. Scared me out of a year's growth. What're you young'uns doing down there?"

"We're trapped," Tim croaked.

"And starving," added Stuffy hoarsely.

"Tell him I found Bootsie."

Debbie's voice was less than a whisper. Tim felt sorry for her. While they waited for Mr. Perkins to bring help, Debbie discovered six newborn kittens in an overturned storage basket and couldn't even squeal.

"So that's why Bootsie wouldn't answer you," said Tim. He remembered Mr. Perkins' wink when he'd said he was sure Bootsie hadn't left the courtyard. The old rancher had known all along.

"Let's eat while we're waiting," said Stuffy.

He dropped one kernel of corn into Tim's hand, one into Debbie's, and popped the last in his own mouth. When they'd cracked the tiny kernels and swallowed, Stuffy grinned.

"And that, *amigos,* is the last of the padres' treasure."

Before Tim could demand an explanation, his mother and father shouted from above ground.

"Tim! Debbie! Are you all right?"

They lined up for inspection. Then the questions turned from worried ones about injuries to those of anger. What were they doing there? Didn't they know better? Why did they worry people like this? Just wait until they got out.

Tim sighed and almost wished one of them had broken a leg, so his parents would stay worried and not get mad.

Debbie found voice enough to moan, "We'll catch it when we get out."

Stuffy grinned. "I'm glad my father is on duty."

The Bowdys moved away and called to someone. A round brown face peered down at them.

"Ramón," demanded Stuffy's father. "What are you doing down there?"

The boy's shoulders lifted in a tired shrug. "Nothing."

Mr. Bowdy shouted to them to move away from the opening. They returned to the storage baskets while shovels crunched and scraped. Debbie cooed over the new kittens while Bootsie paraded around as if no other cat had ever had any before.

"Now what was that about treasure?" asked Tim.

Stuffy patted the cat as he explained. "Do you remember what the priests told the altar boy?"

"Yes, that the treasure belonged to the Papagos if the priests didn't return."

"If they didn't return by spring. Spring is the planting season. What could be a greater treasure to farmers, which the Pima and Papagos have always been, than a store of seed corn?"

Debbie made a raspy noise that passed for a groan. "It's the prospector and the water all over again," she whispered.

She was right. It was the Papagos who'd said the padres left a treasure. What was a treasure to them two hundred years ago wasn't the same as a treasure today.

"Some of these baskets may have had other grain or perhaps apricot and peach pits. Who knows? But this," Stuffy waved his hand, "this, I am sure, was the treasure of the padres. The bell proves it."

"All that digging," said Tim, "and what do we have?"

"Six kittens and a bell," whispered Debbie.

Her voice wasn't returning like Tim's and Stuffy's. But then she'd always yelled a lot more than anybody else to begin with. Her voice was half worn out before they'd started calling for help.

"But Mr. Perkins doesn't have a treasure to show."

"Perhaps not," said Stuffy. "But now that the ghost bell has been found, his mission will be finished quickly."

"I still wish we'd found something important that people would hear about and come to see."

Idly Tim flicked a pebble at the bell. The ringing faded into silence. The steady rasp of the shovels and picks was silent.

"Timothy," yelled Mr. Bowdy. "Are you responsible for that?"

Tim moved to the enlarged hole. "Yes, sir. We found the bell and the treasure, too, if you can call it that."

"What treasure? Never mind. Just stand back."

The men worked twice as fast after that. In a short time Mr. Bowdy slid down into the cave and helped them out. The kittens went up first, then Debbie. Mr. Ramirez hauled Stuffy out next.

"Go on, son," Mr. Bowdy said. "I want to take a look at this bell. Mr. Perkins has brought out the chuck wagon, and supper's ready."

It wasn't a real chuck wagon but the back of Mr. Perkins' truck. He'd made a fast trip home and had enough to feed everyone. Tim matched Stuffy bite for bite. They still weren't finished when the Papago workers drove off after promising to return Monday prepared to camp out during the week.

"Now, young man," said Mrs. Bowdy, "tell us what happened and where you've been all day."

With Debbie unable to speak above a whisper, Tim told the whole story. He got the lecture he expected when he told of entering the cave without telling anyone, but when he came to the part where Debbie screamed at the bats, Dad surprised him with a yell.

"I knew there was a logical explanation," he shouted. "Do you know, Deborah, that you scream like a banshee? You frightened the workers so badly, they spilled a wheelbarrow of broken adobes getting out of the mission. I'll admit I was right behind them. It's a shock to hear something like that rise up from beneath your feet."

"Stuffy thinks there's an entrance to the cave from the mission," Tim said.

"We'll have a look tomorrow. Now everyone home to bed."

Tim was too tired to do more than mutter good night to Stuffy, but when Debbie dragged the basketful of kittens into their room, he found strength enough to yell, "Keep those dumb cats on your own side of the curtain."

Then he tumbled into bed, stretched out his aching legs and arms, and fell asleep.

A heavy weight lay on his chest. He knew it must be morning but he fought against losing the comfort of sleep.

"Some alarm clock," he muttered. "Go away."

Something soft patted his nose and cheek. Tim opened his eyes and stared into two round yellow ones. Bootsie chirruped delightedly at her success.

"Debbie! Get this dumb cat out of here." No one stirred on the other side of the screen. Tim pushed Bootsie off his chest, sat up, and fell back with a groan. Nobody could ache like this and live. He was content to hobble around the house and patio that day. He learned from his father that Stuffy was just as sore and too stiff to ride Chiquita over for a visit.

Debbie, outside of her voice, didn't seem to suffer at all, but even the whisper rose to a full-strength screech when she discovered that evening what was in the first half of the cave.

"Mummies! How absolutely disgusting!"

"Not to the archaeologists," said Mr. Bowdy. "They'll be swarming all over the place in a few days. Evidently the ancient Indians used that cave as a sort of cemetery."

"You mean those big jars and baskets were burial urns like we saw at the museum?"

His father nodded. Tim glowed. People would certainly flock to see that, especially since Mr. Perkins refused to let the mummies be removed.

"He'll let them take photographs and study them," said Mr. Bowdy, "but he wants the mummies to remain where they are. Says they have a right to peace."

"I guess the priests felt the same way. That's why they built the wall."

"Probably, although they wouldn't have wanted anyone coming along the ledge, the way you did, and discovering the treasure."

The next morning Tim was hobbling over to Mr. Perkins' to see the new display cases when he spotted a familiar brown-and-black animal plodding toward the house.

Stuffy winced as he slid to the ground. "Did you hear about the entrance they found to the cave?"

"No, where is it?"

"Under the altar. They discovered it this morning."

As they walked slowly to Mr. Perkins' ramada Tim told about the reporter from the *Tucson Daily Citizen.*

"They're going to do one feature article on the mission bell and another on the mummies and things. It will certainly help Mr. Perkins."

Debbie was helping the rancher place the Indian collection in the cases. One was already filled. Mr. Perkins switched on the lights and stood back proudly.

"How she look?" he asked.

"Just like a real museum," said Tim.

Stuffy grinned. "My mother won't like that basket set out like that."

The Clumsy Finger was propped on edge in the center of the most prominent shelf. Tim smiled at it, then frowned.

"Stuffy, does part of the design remind you of something? Step back and squint your eyes a little."

"It looks like the design on the map. Why, those are the altar steps!"

"And this line must mean underneath or something," said Tim. "This center blob could be the bell if you stretch your imagination a little, and these are the storage jars."

"I'll be jiggered," said Mr. Perkins. "No wonder that old Papago woman told Grandma this basket was valuable. The map's been right under my nose all my life."

"Perhaps even the old woman didn't know what it was," said Stuffy. "The altar boy must have told about the cave and it was woven into a basket as a record, just as knotted strings once kept our history. And like the knotted strings, everyone forgot what it meant."

Tim groaned. "All that trouble and all these aches just because the Papagos didn't have better memories."

"What about you, Timothy Bowdy?" snapped Debbie. "I saw you with this basket right in your hands the day we met Stuffy. Why didn't you figure it out?"

"Oh, for criminy's sake, who thinks about an old basket being a map? Even now we wouldn't know what it was if we hadn't figured out the other map."

"And found the treasure," added Stuffy.

Debbie giggled. "I'll bet it's the first time anyone ever found the treasure before the map."

"We're about as dumb as that cat of yours," Tim admitted. "Come on, Stuffy, Let's ride out to the mission."

"It stormed last night."

Patiently Tim waited for Stuffy to explain. "And?"

"The floods have gone down and almost anything can be found in the washes and arroyos."

"Treasure?"

Stuffy grinned. "Perhaps. I think many things can be treasure. It depends on who finds it."

"And how much he needs it."

Debbie trailed them outside, stepping carefully around the clumps of grass.

"Would you like to come?" Stuffy asked her. "Chiquita can carry three."

"You won't get me on that animal. She's too big."

"Scarebaby." But Tim's tone was teasing instead of scornful. He'd never forget the way he'd felt in that cave, even though Dad had explained that many people felt as he had when closed in a small space. "Come on, Stuffy. Let's go."

The summer stretched before them, more precious than gold.

About the Author

Betty Baker's first published work for Harper was LITTLE RUNNER OF THE LONGHOUSE, An I CAN READ Book about the Iroquois Indians' New Year's celebration. This was followed by THE SHAMAN'S LAST RAID, a humorous story about present-day Apache twins, whereas KILLER-OF-DEATH deals with the serious problems of a young Apache brave in the nineteenth century. KILLER-OF-DEATH received the 1963 Western Heritage Award for the best western children's book of the year.

Betty Baker was born in Bloomsburg, Pennsylvania, has lived in various cities in New Jersey, and now makes her home in Tucson, Arizona, with her husband, Robert Venturo, and their son, Christopher.